Mail Order Misfortune
Book 14 in Brides of Beckham
Kirsten Osbourne

Chapter One

ANNA SIMMONS LEANED back in her chair in the schoolroom and let out a sigh of relief. It was finally over. She'd been teaching in the little schoolroom outside of Beckham, Massachusetts for two years, and she wasn't going to go back. She couldn't. There had to be another job she could take. She loved children, but she hated teaching, and she just couldn't keep doing it indefinitely.

She had enough money saved up that she could continue to pay her room and board to the family she'd lived with for a few more months until she found another job. There had to be something she could do that didn't involve teaching. It wasn't that she didn't like children, because she did. She just didn't feel like teaching was her calling. She hated disciplining the children, and even more, she hated trying to force them to learn things they had no interest in.

At her little school, there was a group of siblings that obviously were not disciplined at all at home. They were so bad, it was almost impossible for Anna to teach, and they'd taken what little joy she'd had from teaching away from her, so now there was only frustration left.

She shook her head. No, she was finished teaching, and no one was ever going to be able to convince her to go back to it. She gathered up the last of her things and erased the chalkboard, happy to know it was the last time ever her hands would be covered with chalk dust. She was thrilled to be closing the book on this chapter of her life and starting another, whatever it may be.

She locked the schoolhouse behind her and walked the two miles to town without ever looking back. She was not going to miss a single thing about teaching. Why women wanted to do it year after year was beyond her comprehension. She wanted to spend her life with a man she loved. Not spend it in a schoolroom forcing disobedient children to learn. She wouldn't do it ever again.

When she reached town, she wasn't certain where to start, so she went into the mercantile and slowly walked up to the owner. She'd always been excessively shy, and having to talk to strangers made her tongue swell in her mouth. She'd talked to Mr. Stanley many times over the years, but still, every time she saw him again, she had to start all over.

She did her best not to mumble as she spoke to him. "Mr. Stanley? Are you hiring?" It was hard for her to get the words out. How was she supposed to ask for a job when she could barely talk around strangers?

The middle aged man looked her up and down. "Why you looking for work? Need something to do for the summer?" He knew she'd been teaching for the past two years, so he was obviously surprised at her question.

She shook her head. "No, sir. I'm not going back to teaching." It was the first time she'd said the words aloud, and she was surprised at how powerful they made her feel.

He frowned. "I don't have work for you. Teaching's the best job for a single lady." He waved to the bulletin board at the back of the store. "Sometimes folks will put their jobs on the bulletin board so people looking for work can find it. Sometimes not. I don't know what's up there now."

Anna nodded and whispered, "Thank you," before heading back over to read the notices. There were more than she'd imagined there would be. Most were people looking for farm hands and such. She slowly read each one. Only one really had potential and that one meant she would be a cook for a local wealthy family. She could do that. They wanted professional cooking experience, but what could be better than cooking in an orphanage?

As she was about to leave, another advertisement caught her eye, this one printed professionally. She picked it up and pocketed it, preferring the idea of working as a cook, but knowing she would come back to it if she needed to. She wasn't too proud to do what she needed to do to survive.

She walked the few blocks to the wealthy side of town to talk to the family looking for a cook, hoping they would at least give her a chance. She knew if anyone would just let her try to cook for them, she would have the job. Getting an interview and a chance would be the hard part.

The family looking for the cook had just hired one, and told her she really didn't have the kind of experience they needed anyway.

She walked to the small park across the street from the family's house and pulled the other advertisement out of her skirt pocket and slowly read it. "Mail Order Bride agency needs women who are looking for the adventure of their lives. Men out West need women to marry. Reply in person at 300 Rock Creek Road. See Miss Elizabeth Miller." She shuddered as she read the name Miller, but surely the family she knew couldn't be related to a woman who owned a mail order bride agency.

Anna read the words three times before she realized they weren't going to change before her eyes. Did she really have the courage to go and talk to a total stranger and ask if she could be a mail order bride? And then would she be able to *be* a mail order bride? She really wasn't certain. It was hard enough to just speak to a man, let alone marry one she'd never met.

She got to her feet and noted the address, knowing she had to do it immediately or she would lose the courage to do it at all. She walked through the quiet streets to Rock Creek Road, just two blocks over from the house she was starting at.

When she reached the house in question, she bowed her head and said a quick prayer, before rushing up the sidewalk to the front door. She knocked and waited impatiently, wishing she'd taken the time to change into her Sunday dress instead of just wearing one of her school dresses. She looked down and saw chalk dust all over her skirt. She was just about to turn away and return the following day when the door opened.

A tall blond man greeted her. "May I help you?" he asked.

If not for the formal butler clothes, the man looked as if he should be in a boxing ring. Even with his suit on, she couldn't help but notice how thick his muscles were. "I'm here to see Elizabeth Miller," she mumbled.

He nodded, opening the door wider and inviting her inside. "Your name, miss?"

She swallowed hard, wishing she wasn't so nervous around men. "It's Simmons. Anna Simmons."

"Right this way, Miss Simmons." He led her toward the back of the house to a room where a young lady sat at a desk. She had blond hair and green eyes, and stood when the door opened. "Miss Anna Simmons is here to see you, Miss Miller."

Elizabeth smiled. "Thank you for showing her in, Bernard. Would you bring us some tea and cookies please?" She turned to Anna and smiled. "Please have a seat. I hope you like tea."

Anna nodded as she walked to the sofa. "I do like tea." She crossed her hands in her lap and gave all her attention to Elizabeth. She had no idea what to say, so she hoped the other woman would begin the conversation and save her the embarrassment. She just couldn't form her thoughts into a sentence.

Elizabeth seemed to be waiting for something, but after a moment she asked, "Are you here about the mail order bride advertisement?"

Anna blushed and nodded. Only a ninny wouldn't announce why she was there first thing. Why was she always a ninny? "Yes, I am."

"Tell me why you want to be a bride," Elizabeth said, taking her seat again at the chair in front of the desk and giving Anna her full attention.

Anna shrugged. "I was raised in the orphanage here in town, and I am too old to live there now, of course. So, I became a teacher, and I've been teaching for two years now. I hate it. I love children, but I hate teaching. I looked to see if there were any jobs for women in town, but there was only one for a cook, and the position is filled, and I really wasn't qualified anyway." Anna knew she was rambling, but she couldn't seem to stop. "So I saw your advertisement for a mail order bride, and thought that might work for me, but I'm so terribly shy, I'm not even certain that would work. I feel like there's something wrong with me that I can't talk to people at all, and here I am just saying anything that comes to mind, and I feel like an idiot."

Elizabeth smiled. "You're not an idiot. It's got to be hard to be so shy and to be totally alone in the world." She turned and looked through her stack of letters, finding one halfway down and handing it to her. "I think Tom would be good for you. He lives outside a small town in Texas, and he's a rancher there."

Anna read through his letter quickly. "Dear Elizabeth, I'm looking for a bride, as I'm sure are most people who write to you. I'm not particular about looks, but I would like to have a woman who is willing to work hard. I have a relatively large spread outside of Wiggieville, Texas, and I need someone who is willing to take care of my home and cook my meals. I'm easy to get along with, and I have enough money to support a wife, but there's not a lot left over at this point. I've taken over my ranch from my parents who moved back East. Please find me a bride who doesn't mind hard work, and is happy to live in the middle of nowhere. Thank you, Tom Harding."

Anna read the letter one more time before nodding. "I think he's fine. What do I do now?" She felt her hand shaking nervously at the idea of responding to this man, but she knew it was the right thing for her future.

Elizabeth handed her a pencil and a sheet of crisp white paper. "Write him a letter. Tell him about yourself, and we'll take it from there."

Anna nodded, putting pencil to paper. "Dear Tom, I live in Beckham, Massachusetts, and I think I'd be a good wife to you. I'm a good cook, and I really don't mind cleaning. I would be a hard-working wife. I'm incredibly shy, though, so you'd have to be patient with me. I might even try to turn tail and run home once I get there. I've never been comfortable around men, but if you can handle that, I'm happy to marry you. I'm twenty-years-old, and I would be happy to live in the middle of nowhere, keeping house and raising a family. Sincerely, Anna Simpson."

She handed the letter to Elizabeth, waiting while she read it. Elizabeth said nothing as she sealed and addressed the letter. "It usually takes about two weeks to receive a response. Once I have, I'll contact you, and we'll talk." She leaned back in her chair. "Did you grow up here in Beckham?"

"Yes, I grew up in the orphanage here in town. My father died in the War Between the States, and my Mama died of the fever a few weeks after I was born." She shrugged. "There was no family left to care for me, so a neighbor dropped me at the orphanage." She'd told the story many times, and she wasn't sad about it, but she felt like something was wrong because she wasn't. Should she be sad about a family she had no memory of?

Elizabeth sighed. "I'm sorry."

"What about you? Did you grow up here?" Anna leaned back on the sofa, at ease for the first time in a long while. She'd lived as a boarder while teaching and didn't know the family well. She had no real friends outside of the orphans she'd grown up with, and they'd all moved off and had lives of their own.

"Yes, I did. I grew up on a farm outside town. My sister was a mail order bride a few years back. She settled in Texas near Fort Worth." She frowned. "I wish I could travel out with you and visit her for a while. I haven't seen Susan since she married."

"Is Susan happy?" Anna couldn't help but worry that she was making a terrible mistake moving somewhere where she knew no one to marry a stranger.

Elizabeth nodded. "Oh, yes! She's very happy. She has four step-sons and three children of her own. We write every week."

"Seven children? Oh my. Your parents didn't mind her going to Texas to marry a stranger?"

"Not really. Susan wasn't happy at home. Our younger brothers and sisters are called 'the demon horde' around town." Elizabeth shook her head as if trying to deny her own words.

Anna's eyes widened. "I had six of your siblings in school this year!" She tried not to shudder visibly at the thought of them.

Elizabeth grinned, nodding to the butler as he came in and set down a tray with tea and cookies before leaving the room, closing the door behind him. "They've certainly earned their name, haven't they?"

Anna nodded emphatically. "They're a great deal of the reason I've decided to quit teaching." After she said the words, she wondered if she'd gone too far. Would Elizabeth be offended and not help her?

"I'm not surprised. I can't wait to write Susan and tell her, though." Elizabeth grinned. "They really are monsters. They always have been."

"It's hard to believe one of the demon horde could grow up to run her own business. Do all of you have both of the same parents?" She couldn't imagine the woman in front of her once being one of the wild children who wreaked such havoc in the local school.

"Oh, yes," Elizabeth answered. "Mother was much better about discipline when there were only four of us. It's the younger ones that were spoiled so horribly."

"I see." Anna didn't really, though. All children were treated the same when they were in an orphanage. She didn't have any experience with having parents, though.

"I wish I did," Elizabeth said with a laugh. "Where will you stay through the summer? I assume you board with a family near the schoolhouse?"

Anna nodded. "I only spend enough money to keep myself clothed adequately. I have money saved, and I'll continue to pay for my room and board until it's time for me to go." She should be able to make herself a new wardrobe as well, but she didn't add that. Being raised to a life of frugality came in very handy when living on a teacher's salary.

"Good." Elizabeth poured them each a cup of tea and handed a cup and a plate of cookies to Anna. "Do you like the family you board with?"

Anna shrugged. "They're fine. I don't really know them well. I spend my time in my bedroom working on lesson plans and grading papers. I help with the dishes and eat meals with them, but that's about it." She knew she should have made more of an effort to get to know the family, but for her it truly was an effort, and she had no desire to work that hard at home.

Elizabeth frowned. "Have you tried to get to know them?"

Anna shook her head. "I don't do well with strangers, although I seem to be comfortable with you. I'm not certain why."

Elizabeth gave Anna a half smile, obviously concerned about her. "How will you spend your summer?"

"I'll sew and get things ready for my journey west. I know I'll need more clothes than what I have and a few good aprons." Anna was glad she wouldn't be starting her marriage with children. She didn't need to have that added stress as she got to know a man. She would be scared enough as she was. At least Tom sounded like a good loving man.

"Have you thought about meeting someone here at home and not going out West to be a bride?" Elizabeth asked.

"I have a hard time talking to men. I don't know how I'd get to the point of even being courted let alone married." Anna shook her head. "No, I'll take my chances on a stranger."

JESSE LEFT ERNIE WITH the housekeeper he'd hired after Deborah's death and walked down to the graveyard to visit his wife. She'd been gone for three years, and still, he thought about her every day. She'd been the only woman he'd ever met who'd been worth giving up his freedom for. He'd loved her more than he'd ever thought possible, and since she'd been gone, he only felt as if he were half a man.

He sank down onto the grass beside her grave and spoke to her. "Oh, Deborah, I don't know what to do. Ernie is known all around the area as a hellion. He's only eight and already he's in trouble every day in school." He set the cup of flowers he'd put on her grave just the day before back up, and picked some of the weeds from her grave. "My housekeeper says she's going to quit at the end of the month. She can't handle him any longer. He's been expelled from school three different times now. You kept him behaving just the way he should, but I don't think anyone else could do it the way you did."

His fingers traced over her name on her tombstone. "My papa died. He left me money, a lot more money than I realized he had. I think I'm going to take that money and go buy a ranch in Texas." He sighed. "You know I've always dreamed of owning a ranch out West, and I found a great opportunity. An older couple is going to sell their ranch, and they're including furniture as well as the cattle. Most of the cowboys will even stay on. I don't know what else to do, and I think we need a fresh start. Of course, that means I won't get to see you anymore, but I'll always love you. I promise. I need to do this for Ernie as much as for me. I wish I could explain just how bad it's gotten, but I don't know how. I'll find a housekeeper out there who doesn't know what he's like, and she'll be able to keep him in line." He stood up, tears filling his dark eyes. "I love you, Deborah. Don't forget it."

He made the fifteen minute walk home from the graveyard, feeling as if he had his answer. When he'd told Deborah it was time to move on, he had felt an overwhelming sense of peace come over him, as if she approved of his plans. Yes, moving to Texas was the answer. He hoped he could get Mrs. Jenkins to stay long enough to help him pack everything up.

"YOU HAVE A GUEST," Mrs. Roper said, moving aside so that Anna could leave her room.

It had been six weeks since Anna had talked to Elizabeth Miller, and she'd been sewing diligently ever since. Her things were almost ready for her to leave, taking the train to Texas. She'd heard a lot about how wild Texas was, and she was more than a little frightened, but she was getting everything in order so she could leave as soon as she received his letter.

She stepped into the small parlor and found Elizabeth waiting for her. Anna smiled. "Hello." She clenched her fists nervously, wondering what news the other woman had brought her.

Elizabeth looked at her, beaming. "You received a letter today, so I brought it by."

Anna took the letter and sat down beside Elizabeth on the sofa. She carefully opened it and read it. "Dear Anna, You sound like just the bride for me. I'll be waiting for you at the stagecoach here in Wiggieville. I've included train tickets to depart on August seventeenth, and then there will be a stagecoach to catch once you get to Weatherford, Texas. I know your journey will be long, so I've included some money for food along the way. I look forward to seeing you. We'll marry as soon as you step off the stagecoach. Once you get here, I'm not letting you get away from me."

She took the cash and tickets from the letter and gave the bank draft that was included to Elizabeth. "He wants me to leave tomorrow.

I don't think I can do that! I'm not ready!" She could barely breathe just thinking about leaving the following day. She just couldn't do it.

Elizabeth frowned. "Well, we may be able to get the train station to switch your ticket for you, and then we can send a telegram to Tom letting him know that you'll be a little late. When do you think you can go?"

Anna thought about it for a moment. It really wasn't about being physically ready to go. She'd done more than enough sewing, and it would only take her an hour to pack up everything she owned. She just needed time to prepare mentally for the journey. "Two weeks?"

Elizabeth nodded. "I don't think that's excessive." She stood. "I brought my horse and buggy. Why don't we drive into town, and I'll help you switch your ticket and send a telegram to Tom. It shouldn't be a problem."

The ticket was exchanged, and they went to the telegraph office. Because she was frugal, and had to pay by the letter, Anna carefully crafted her message. "TH I will be arriving two weeks later than scheduled stop I hope you will forgive me for making everyone wait stop Miss Simmons stop"

Elizabeth nodded in agreement. "That should work beautifully." She tucked her arm through Anna's as they walked back to the buggy. "I'll pick you up the morning of the thirty-first, and drive you to the train station myself. I like to have a talk with everyone before they depart."

Anna nodded, relieved. She hadn't looked forward to carrying her trunk into town by herself, and she certainly didn't feel like she could ask Mr. Roper to take her into town. She hated to ask anyone for anything after growing up an orphan. "I'd like that a lot."

Elizabeth smiled. "Your train leaves at noon, so I'll be by around half past ten to make sure we get everything loaded on time, and we make it to the station."

"That sounds good. I'll be ready and waiting for you." Anna was thrilled to have the extra two weeks to ready herself mentally. She would need every minute of each day.

THE MORNING OF THE thirty-first was beautiful and sunny. Anna was glad her last day in her hometown of twenty years would be pretty for her. Elizabeth arrived exactly on time and helped Anna load her trunk into the back of the buggy. Anna also carried a small carpet bag with everything she'd need while on the journey.

She climbed into the buggy beside Elizabeth, and they talked the entire way into town. "I don't know if I told you the story of how I came to be the owner of the bride agency," Elizabeth began. Anna shook her head. "I told you my sister was a bride who had left Beckham. Harriett Long was the owner back then, and she placed Susan with her husband. A few years later, I came into town one day and happened to overhear that Harriett was leaving town and would be closing the agency."

Anna looked at her in surprise. "Closing it? But it's open!"

"I know. I told her I thought Beckham needed an agency to help women find husbands. I felt like she did a great service. So Harriett invited me to run the business. She taught me everything there was to know about running it, and then she went off to be a mail order bride herself in Seattle. The house is really hers. I don't see her ever coming back for it, but legally, it belongs to her."

"I had no idea. I don't know what I thought, but that certainly wasn't it." She admired Elizabeth for being willing to stand up for something she believed in. She'd never had the courage to do that herself.

"No, I understand. As part of taking over the business, I promised that I would always have a very important talk with the brides before they left. Never let a man mistreat you. As women, we're in a bad position if we marry a bad man. Men can beat their wives and no one thinks anything of it. Promise me that if you end up in a bad situation, you will let me know. In return, I promise that I will send you a train ticket, and I will let you stay with me until you're back on your feet."

Anna thought about it for a moment. She'd never thought about men beating their wives, but she could see that it was a possibility. Finally she nodded. "I won't stay in a bad situation."

Elizabeth smiled and nodded. "That's what I needed to hear. I packed you enough food for today on the train. You'll want to save every dime you can along the way." She stopped in front of the train station, and together they got the trunk out of the buggy. Elizabeth hugged Anna tightly. "I'll wait with you until they call your train, but I want to hug you now. I don't do the 'crying as I watch people pull out' thing. It makes me too sad. I need you to write me as soon as you're settled in Wiggieville. I hope you have a wonderful time there!"

Anna nodded, shaking a little now that the time to leave was at hand. She'd spend ten days on a train and then a few hours on a stage coach. It was going to be a long trip, and she'd never been further from home than an hour out into the country.

They waited, side by side, for the train to be called, chatting about different things in town. Elizabeth told some stories about Texas that her sister had sent, and even told her about how her two older step-sons had gotten into a fight and rolled around in mud on her wedding day.

The stories helped Anna relax and made her laugh. She hadn't had a lot in her life worth laughing about, but she decided then that she would do her best to laugh more. Everyone needed to smile. She would be a joyful wife for Tom, because he sounded like the kind of man that deserved a joyful wife.

Chapter Two

ANNA FELT A MOMENT of panic as she searched for her stagecoach at the train station in Weatherford, Texas. She was so close to the end of her journey, and she just wanted to be there. Yes, she knew she would be marrying a stranger at the end of the journey, but by that point, she was so tired, she didn't even care as long as he had a bed she could sleep in.

She found her coach and climbed in, sitting with her hands folded primly in her lap as she stared out the window. She waited for someone else to join her, but there was no one else. She would be alone for the long drive to Wiggieville. She wished that Tom would have arrived to get her at the train station, but she understood that he probably couldn't take the time away from work to meet her there.

When they pulled into Wiggieville, Anna looked around the small town. There was a mercantile, a church, a school, several houses, and not much more. She climbed down using the step the driver put down and waited as he took the trunk down from atop the stage. He'd pulled away before she let herself look around for Tom. He'd said he'd be there waiting for her, but she was slightly worried he hadn't received her telegram.

There was no one waiting. No one at all. He wouldn't have just forgotten about her, would he? She could feel her heart beating faster, and her breath was coming too quickly. She was in a state far from home and knew no one. If he didn't come to meet her, she had no idea what she'd do.

Anna was starting to panic, tears filling her eyes when a red headed woman stopped her buggy beside her.

"Are you here to meet someone?" the lady asked, her voice soft and sweet.

Anna nodded. "I'm here to meet my fiancé, Tom Harding. He was supposed to be waiting for me." She hoped the woman in front of her knew Tom and could take her to him. Maybe he'd been injured while working his ranch. Anything could have happened to him. She found she wasn't as worried about Tom as she was about what she'd do if she couldn't find him.

"Come with me. We'll talk." Anna put her things into the back of the buggy and climbed up to sit beside her. "My name is Julia."

"I'm Anna Simmons." She hated talking to a stranger this way, but she didn't feel like she had a choice. She needed to find her fiancé so she wouldn't be alone here in a strange place.

"I was Julia Simmons until two weeks ago. I'm going to tell you a funny story." Anna nodded, her face skeptical. "When I arrived in Wiggieville two weeks ago, I was expecting someone from the school board to be waiting for me. A man walked up to me, and asked if I was 'Miss Simmons.' I, of course, said I was, and he kissed me. Right there in the middle of the street. I had heard people were friendlier in Texas, but that was a lot friendlier than what I was expecting. I very politely asked him to take me to wherever I was staying. He said that was fine, but he had to make a stop first. His stop was the preacher's house. When I realized he intended to marry me, I tried to explain that I was here to teach school, not to marry him, but every time I protested, he'd just start kissing me again. Before I knew it, I was standing in front of the preacher, and he was pronouncing us husband and wife. And that's how I ended up married to your fiancé."

Anna felt her heart drop into her stomach. "I can certainly understand how that could have happened. I told him I was certain that once I arrived, I would just try to run back home, so he must have just kept kissing you to keep you from running away." She shrugged. "I'm not upset, because he was a stranger to me, but I don't know what I'm supposed to do now." Was there a boarding house in town where she could stay until she found a job? Were there even jobs for women like her?

Julia smiled warmly. "Well, I think there's only one answer. You go home with me."

"So what's Tom like?" Anna asked, her mind franticly wondering if the solution would work. How could she just move in with her former fiancé and his wife? It just wouldn't be right. They were still newlyweds.

Julia grinned. "He's a wonderful husband to me. I honestly couldn't ask for a better man. I'm still teaching until another teacher can be found, and he's been very supportive of me throughout it all."

"Will he mind that you're bringing me home with you?" What man would want a stranger living with him and his new wife? No, Tom wouldn't want her there.

Julia shook her head. "No, of course not. He'll understand that he's the one who stranded you by marrying me, so it's our responsibility to help you. We have a spare room that you can use until you decide what you want to do." Her voice was strong and confident. She seemed determined to take Anna home with her.

Anna bit her lip. She didn't have a lot of choices, but she didn't want to take advantage of the other woman's generosity. "I guess I really have nowhere to go, do I?"

"We would buy you a ticket back home if you need us to, or there are plenty of unmarried men around. You could stay with us until you found one you were interested in marrying. Or you don't happen to be a certified teacher do you?" Julia asked the question flippantly, but she seemed to really want an answer.

Anna looked at her in surprise. "I was a teacher before I left home. Why? Does this town need a teacher now?" She didn't want to go back to teaching, but it was better than being stuck in a town she didn't know having to live with people she didn't know. She couldn't think of anything worse than that. At least she'd have her own income.

"They don't allow married women to teach here, so I'm just working until they find someone to replace me. If you wanted to teach, you would have a place to stay, because there was a family in town who had agreed to let me board there."

Anna nodded, reluctant to teach again, but knowing she really didn't have a choice at that point. "Could you introduce me to the school board at church on Sunday? If you don't mind that is."

"Oh, I don't mind at all. Mr. Hanson will be pleased to have someone interested in the post, because he's very eager to get rid of me." Julia shrugged. "He really has a problem with a married woman teaching, but I'm not certain why. I've never really understood why a married woman can't be as good of a teacher as an unmarried woman. I'd think a married woman would be more focused on the students and not thinking nearly as much about who she's going to marry."

"I'm not certain I understand the reasoning either, but I do know it's a rule in most places." Anna stared at the brown grass that seemed to go on forever. Didn't it ever rain in Texas? "How far is it to the ranch?"

"We're almost there. Tom doesn't know you're coming, so be prepared for him to be surprised. He never got your telegram, you know. It went to Mr. Hanson, because you just used initials, and Tom and Mr. Hanson have the same initials." Julia smiled at her.

"I guess I did everything wrong, didn't I? If I'd gotten on that train the day I was supposed to instead of being too afraid to leave town, none of this ever would have happened." Anna shook her head, disgusted with herself. She should have done as she said she would instead of inventing reasons to wait.

"Oh, is that why you were late?" Julia parked in front a house and carefully stepped down. "If you want to leave your bags, Tom will happily take them in for you when he unhitches the horse."

Anna nodded, just taking her small carpet bag inside, but leaving her trunk for Tom to carry. It was the least he could do after marrying someone else, right?

She followed Julia inside to the kitchen where the other woman hurriedly began cooking. Anna pulled her apron on so she could do whatever she could to help her.

Julia smiled. "You don't have to help with supper. Your room is at the top of the stairs. Go ahead and get comfortable."

"Oh, I love to cook," Anna protested. "What are you fixing?" She truly preferred cooking to teaching any day of the week.

Julia shrugged. "I think I'm just going to make stew with some salt pork, and maybe some biscuits to go with it."

"I'll make the biscuits," Anna offered. She made light, fluffy biscuits that never failed to receive a compliment. She'd love to share her cooking with her new friend.

"Did you cook a lot for your family?" Julia asked as she watched her cook.

"I was an orphan, raised in an orphanage in Beckham, Massachusetts. I helped in the kitchen there a great deal. When I was too old to stay any longer, I became a teacher, but I really didn't enjoy it, so I decided to become a mail order bride." She stared down at her hands for a moment. "I should have fulfilled my obligations and just come instead of deciding to wait longer." She wondered how different her life was going to be because of that one decision.

"Honestly? I'm glad you waited. I never would have married Tom if you hadn't, and I'm very happy with him."

Anna smiled, wondering what this perfect man that Julia kept talking about would be like. Would she find him as fascinating as Julia obviously did?

Tom walked into the room then, giving her an odd look as he walked over to kiss Julia. Watching the two of them together, Anna knew she'd done the best thing for everyone concerned. Tom was a large man, and she wanted to immediately cower away from him. She avoided his gaze and kept cooking, looking for an excuse to run up the stairs away from him as soon as she could.

After supper she did just that. She took a bath, in a real bathtub for the first time in her life, before disappearing up the stairs. She thanked God that she'd not married Tom, knowing she never could have been happy with him. Julia was meant to be Tom's bride and God must have other plans for her.

AT CHURCH ON SUNDAY morning, Julia went out of her way to introduce Anna to Mr. Hanson, who seemed like a pompous ninny to Anna.

"So you've taught before? What's your experience?" Mr. Hanson was as wide as he was tall, and had a tendency to sweat. He had sweat dripping down his ruddy cheeks, and Anna wanted to take a step back to avoid getting rained on.

"I taught for two years at a small rural school outside of Beckham, Massachusetts. I boarded with a local family while I taught there," Anna replied, watching his face to see his reaction. She'd never imagined she would be interviewed at church. Why couldn't he set up a time to meet with her like a normal person?

Mr. Hanson nodded importantly. "My wife and I have agreed to board the new teacher, whomever she may be. Our children are out of the house now, but I'm on the school board, and we live just across the street from the schoolhouse."

"That sounds as if it would work for me." Anna dug into the draw string purse she had attached to her wrist. "I brought my teaching credentials in case you needed to see them." She had packed it thinking it might come in handy, but she'd truly hoped she'd never have to use her teaching certificate again.

"This seems to be in order. Yes, absolutely. I'll talk to the others, but I believe we'll be offering you a job. Where are you staying?"

"I'm staying with Julia and Tom Harding. I was supposed to marry Tom," Anna said softly. It felt strange admitting that she was the bride who came too late to marry him, but she held her head up high.

"Yes, I've heard what happened there. It's why I'm looking for a new teacher." He shook his head. "I hope your morals are stronger than the last teacher we hired. We will offer you forty dollars a month for teaching, minus ten dollars a month for room and board. Would that be acceptable should we offer you the position?"

"That sounds more than fair." Anna wanted to kick him for the way he talked about Julia, but what could she really do? The man held her future in the palm of his hand.

Julia shook her head as Mr. Hanson walked off to go speak with the other members of the school board. "He makes me so angry! It's like he doesn't have the ability to remember what it's like to meet someone and be attracted to them."

Anna smiled. "Don't listen to him. He's just trying to do his job, even if he's going about it in a very odd way." She didn't believe a single word she said, of course, but she would be polite if it killed her.

"Oh, I know. I'm working hard to make certain the children are taught well, even though he makes me angry. I'm honestly looking forward to the day when I can be a full-time wife. Teaching here is not what I imagined teaching would be."

Anna patted Julia's arm. "Nothing is ever exactly what you think it will be. I had Tom all built up in my head to be an almost god-like man. I get here, and he's just like every other man I've ever met." She was so relieved that she hadn't married him. Teaching was preferable to marrying a man who intimidated her so much.

Julia laughed. "I had never heard of him, but I think he's pretty wonderful. I guess it's all in the eye of the beholder, isn't it?"

Mr. Hanson came back then, interrupting their giggles. "The school board has voted to offer you the position. You may start tomorrow."

"Tomorrow? That soon? But..." Anna wasn't sure she could be ready to start that quickly. She needed to ready herself mentally to take over the schoolroom.

"Is there a problem with that, Miss Simmons?" Mr. Hanson raised an eyebrow as if just waiting for her to argue with him.

"No, sir." Anna looked at Julia, hoping her friend would help her get ready for the task ahead of her.

"We'll get you packed and take you to Mr. Hanson's house this evening, Anna. It's no problem." Julia squeezed Anna's hand, obviously trying to give her some courage for the job.

"I should think not. It's going to be hard enough for those children to have to switch teachers mid-term. We'll make the transition as smooth as possible." He looked at Julia. "You'll be paid for the half month you worked. Good day."

Anna couldn't believe how rude the man had been. She wasn't looking forward to staying with him at all. What if he treated his wife that way? She would be morally obligated to hit him over the head with a frying pan. She wasn't certain she'd be able to stop herself.

JESSE WAS EXHAUSTED by the time he and Ernie finally reached Wiggieville, Texas. It was an odd name for a town, but he hoped the place would be just what Ernie needed to settle down and start acting like he should.

One of the first things he did on Saturday morning was go to the mercantile with Ernie in tow. "Do you happen to know of any women looking for work? Maybe a widow who's a good cook and enjoys cleaning, but her family has moved on?" He said a quick prayer that there would be someone meeting his description. There was no way he could run a ranch, cook, clean, and run herd on Ernie. He needed someone to help him fast.

The owner shook his head. "Out here when a man dies, another man marries his lady within a week or two. We don't have any single women, 'cept the school teacher, of course, but she ain't allowed to marry."

Jesse nodded tiredly as he bought the supplies they needed. "So there's a school?" That was a plus. He would have somewhere to send Ernie during the week.

"Oh, yes. Miss Simmons is the teacher, and she's a pretty little thing. Never talks above a whisper far as I can tell, but she's a good teacher."

Jesse looked down at Ernie. "You hear that? You'll be starting school on Monday." It would be easy to have him start school in a new place where no one knew of his mischief. Jesse was relieved to hear the town had a school. He'd heard that many didn't out West.

"I don't want to go to school, Pa. I want to stay home with you and help on the ranch."

The mercantile owner's eyes perked up. "You buy the old Kyle ranch?"

Jesse nodded. "I did. I start work first thing Monday morning." He wished he had the energy to start immediately, because the place really needed it, but he didn't. He had to take the weekend to rest. Besides, the preacher had already invited him to dinner on Sunday night. He was looking forward to going.

"It's a good spread. Shocked us all when Kyle announced he was retiring and moving back East." The man continually wiped the same spot on his counter until Jesse wanted to warn him he was going to wipe a hole right through it. What was it about mercantile owners and wiping the same spot all day?

"I was happy to be able to buy it. All the hands are being kind enough to stay, so I'll be able to learn easy." He knew he probably shouldn't admit that he was new at owning a ranch, but he'd done enough reading about it, he was certain he wouldn't make any really stupid mistakes. At least he hoped he wouldn't.

"What about your wife? How's she feel about moving to Texas to be a rancher's wife?"

Jesse shook his head. "My wife died three years back. It's just Ernie and me." He didn't want to elaborate, so he paid for his goods and left, wondering how he was going to be able to cook enough to keep either of them alive. At least the mercantile sold some bread. He could do something with that. Probably.

SETTLING INTO THE HANSON home was easier than Anna had anticipated. Her room was small, but it had everything she needed, and she could easily go in it and shut the door, closing out the Hanson family. She helped Mrs. Hanson with the dishes after each meal, and when Mrs. Hanson wanted help, Anna would help her cook as well. She certainly didn't mind being in the kitchen, but when Mr. Hanson was around, she went to her room and closed him out. He hadn't been nearly as rude to her as he had been to her friend, Julia, but she wasn't going to do anything to get him to be rude. It obviously didn't take much.

School was remarkably easy compared to teaching in Beckham. She still didn't enjoy being a teacher, but without the demon horde attending her school, there were no discipline problems and just students working all day every day. This was what she'd imagined teaching would be, and she wasn't dissatisfied with the turn of events that had brought her back to the classroom. Teaching was fine as long as she wasn't teaching a classroom full of little demon spawn.

She'd been teaching for two weeks without a single incident, and she was starting to relax a bit, feeling more comfortable with the task in front of her.

She was actually looking forward to school Monday morning, and ate her breakfast as quickly as she could without Mr. Hanson making a comment about it. She wiped the dishes dry for Mrs. Hanson, and the two of them spoke in hushed tones as they worked. For some reason, Mr. Hanson thought it was unseemly for women to enjoy housework, and he didn't like them to talk loudly or laugh while they worked. Apparently in his mind, women shouldn't ever do anything they enjoyed.

Anna was comfortable enough with Mrs. Hanson that they often enjoyed their housework when they knew Mr. Hanson was out of the house. Anna wondered how the sweet woman could deal with her husband, but she knew better than to ask. Mrs. Hanson seemed to all but worship Mr. Hanson, and she wasn't about to try and get in the way of marital bliss.

When she finished with the dishes, Anna hurried to her room to get her things for school, taking the lunch pail that Mrs. Hanson provided for her every morning. "I'll see you this afternoon, Mrs. Hanson."

"Have a good day, dear."

Anna rushed out the door, glad to be away from the house where she felt so oppressed. She walked slowly to the schoolyard, looking forward to another week. The children were all so well behaved, she felt like she should send a 'thank you' note to each of their parents for teaching them manners.

She swept out the schoolroom as she did each morning, and was sitting at her desk reading a good book when the children started coming. She would look up and smile or call a greeting as each one put their things on their desk and ran outside to go to play until she called them.

A young boy, no more than eight, that she hadn't seen before came into the schoolhouse and looked around at the empty seats. Anna stood up. "Are you new here? I'm Miss Simmons." She pointed to an empty desk. "That's a good place for you to sit. What's your name?" She was excited at the prospect of a new student, which told her this teaching job really was where she was meant to be.

The boy looked at her, his eyes filled with orneriness. She knew the look well, because every child of the demon horde had that same look every day. "I'm Ernie Hoover. My pa and me just moved here on Saturday."

"Just you and your pa?" she asked, wanting to know about his mother.

"Ma's dead." He said nothing else as he dumped his things on his desk and hurried out to the schoolyard.

Anna sighed. Her sweet two weeks of teaching a well-behaved class were over. She had a hellion, and she was going to have to deal with behavioral issues again. She shook her head. *At least there aren't six of them, right?*

Walking out to the schoolyard, she called the children into class, and they all came running and skipping, many of them already out of breath. Laughter rang through the building, and Anna couldn't help but smile. She didn't like teaching a great deal, but she loved children. Having the chance to interact with them every day made her days better.

She sat down and carefully added Ernie's name to her roster, asking him to come forward for a moment. "You've been to school before?" she asked softly. Not every child had the opportunity to go to school, but she assumed he had by the look on his face that told her he was an experienced mischief-maker.

He nodded sullenly, refusing to even look at her. "Yup."

Anna took a deep breath, knowing that he was being deliberately rude. Most of the children would only respond with, "Yes, ma'am."

"Would you mind showing me where you are in your reader and in arithmetic? I need to know what class to put you in."

Ernie stomped back to his desk and got his books. He showed her his spot in his reader, his eyes daring her to say something about how little he'd accomplished in it. He was further along with his arithmetic.

Anna smiled and nodded. "Thank you, Ernie. You'll be in the second reading group but the third arithmetic group. Please come forward when your classes are called." She wasn't looking forward to the problems he'd cause, but she was determined to treat him just like any other student until he started misbehaving.

Ernie returned to his seat, plopped his books on his desk, and promptly slouched down in his seat, making it clear he didn't want to be there.

Anna sighed. He was going to be a difficult boy. He was showing all the signs already. Ernie was just what she needed to make her school year complete.

BY THE END OF THE WEEK, Ernie had started a fistfight, blocked a younger student into the outhouse so they couldn't get out, came in late after lunch every day, refused to study, and basically tried to make her life as difficult as humanly possible.

She didn't like to have to use the ruler on children's hands, because she found that it interrupted everyone's learning, and that wasn't fair to anyone else. On Friday afternoon of Ernie's first week in school, she penned a note, working hard to be polite. "Dear Mr. Hoover, I would like you to come in after school on Monday to discuss your son's behavior in my classroom. He's been quite disruptive, and I believe we need to work together to make certain we have a plan for the future. Thank you, and I look forward to meeting you. Sincerely, Miss Simmons." *There. Very polite and straight to the point. If that didn't bring the man running, nothing would.*

AFTER SCHOOL ON MONDAY, Anna erased the blackboard as she did every day after school, preparing to write out the next day's tasks for the students. She found if she had everything written out when they arrived at the beginning of the day, they had an easier day with no one asking what to do next.

She was expecting Mr. Hoover any moment, and she was nervous, like she always was when she had to meet a new man. She knew he'd been at church the previous day, because she'd seen Ernie running around outside with the other children, but she hadn't noticed who he was with. She hadn't been there long enough to be able to know which child belonged to which parent.

She heard footsteps behind her and she turned around, looking to see who was there. A man, of medium height and build, with dark hair and brown eyes the color of chocolate stood at the back of the school with his hand clamped firmly on Ernie's shoulder. Her heart skipped a beat as soon as she saw him, and she wondered why she was more nervous around this man than usual. She was usually nervous enough.

She walked toward the back of the room, swallowing hard, because she always had a hard time talking to men, and she was certain this man would be no exception. Once she reached the back of the room, she looked down at Ernie who was squirming under his father's hand. "Go on out to the schoolyard, Ernie. I need to speak with your father privately." She gave him a half smile of encouragement, assuming he was nervous about her speaking privately with his father.

Ernie looked at his father and stuck his tongue out at Anna, before running from the room. Anna waited for Mr. Hoover to say something to correct the boy, but when he didn't, she wanted to scream. "Do you always let him get away with disrespectful behavior, Mr. Hoover?" *No wonder he misbehaves so badly in school if you don't discipline him!*

Mr. Hoover raised an eyebrow before sticking this thumbs through the belt loops of his work pants and looking her up and down. How dare this little mouse think she had the right to tell him how to raise his child? "Do you always let your students treat you disrespectfully and expect their parents to fix the problem? I assure you, Miss Simmons, I don't have time to sit in your classroom all day and do *your* job."

Anna had never been so angry with a man in her entire life, not even Mr. Hanson. Usually, she would be afraid to react to the criticism, but she was furious, and her shyness flew out the window. She took a step toward him, her tiny stature still having to look way up to him despite that fact that he wasn't any taller than average. "If you were doing *your* job and raising the boy right in the first place, he wouldn't dare to think of being disrespectful in *my* classroom!"

"Who do you think you are to tell me I'm not raising my boy right?" He took one more step forward, and the two of them were all but brushing their bodies up against one another as they faced each other. He could see the pores on her nose and the flecks of green in her otherwise sky blue eyes.

"Are you telling me that you don't think you should have to teach your boy to behave correctly in the first place, and it's my job to both parent *and* teach him?" As soon as the words were out of her mouth, she knew she'd gone too far, but she couldn't take them back. She bit her lip, waiting to see what the man would say or do.

Jesse Hoover's eyes flashed as he stared down at the tiny little spitfire of a teacher. He knew Ernie was trouble. He had been ever since his mother had died, but it wasn't Jesse's job to deal with him while Ernie was at school. He was only eight. What kind of teacher couldn't deal with an eight year old boy? "Don't you have a ruler you can use on his knuckles?" He hated the idea of anyone hitting his son, but he knew that was the normal discipline in school rooms. He'd had a ruler used on his own knuckles more times than he could count.

Anna's couldn't believe her ears. "If he was disciplined properly at home, I wouldn't have to resort to corporal punishment in my classroom. If I have to get the ruler out, then I will have to disrupt the entire class to use it. If you will just discipline him at home and make it clear that you will back up whatever I say, then we won't have any more issues!"

Jesse was so angry he wanted to hit the woman. He stared down into her pretty face and realized hitting her wasn't what he wanted to do. He wanted to kiss her. He grabbed her by the waist and pulled her to him, his mouth crushing hers with a hard kiss, his tongue immediately demanding entrance.

Anna stood paralyzed for a moment, not believing this man was actually touching her. Didn't he know she was his son's teacher? It only took a moment for her to feel her stomach fill with longing. She put her hands up to his shoulders to push him away, and instead, she grasped them and clung to him. Her mind was no longer functioning. What was he doing to her?

After a moment, Jesse lifted his head, staring down at the pretty little teacher. Her hair was coming down from the sides of her bun, where it had been pinned up severely. Her lips, a bright pink and moist from his kiss, were still parted, and she was panting slightly. She was a teacher? She looked like she should be a dancer in the local saloon. Not her clothes, of course, but the wanton look on her face. He stared at her for a moment, waiting for her to open her eyes and realize exactly what she was doing.

Anna blinked a few times, returning to reality. Instead of agreeing to discipline his child properly, he had kissed her instead. She had never been kissed before, and the first time she was, it was by a man whose first name she didn't even know. What was wrong with her?

She took a step back, just as she saw the pink fabric of the skirt of a dress disappear around the corner. "Oh blast! Someone just saw that. I'm going to lose my job!" She folded her arms across her chest for a moment, glaring at him, waiting for him to tell her that it would be all right.

Jesse's eyes widened. Why would he care if she lost her job? If she couldn't control Ernie, then she was obviously a terrible teacher anyway. "I guess you shouldn't be going around kissing your students' fathers instead of working then, should you?"

Anna clenched her fists, not believing this man was really blaming her for the kiss *he* initiated. "I trust that you'll talk to Ernie and get his behavior under control so that I don't have to expel him. Good day, Mr. Hoover." She turned and walked regally to her desk on the raised platform at the front of the room, and sank into her chair. He had to leave so she could think. Her mind was racing in a hundred different directions at once.

Why had he kissed her? And more importantly, why had she liked it? Who had seen her, and would they tell? What would she do if she lost her job? She wanted to bury her face in her hands and have a good cry, but she couldn't with him standing there staring at her.

He couldn't believe she was such a little snob, and he wasn't going to deal with her any longer. His son was fine. He was just a boy. That woman was just going to have to learn how to deal with boys. Where had they found her anyway? Didn't they want women who knew how to work with children to teach?

Once in the schoolyard, he grabbed Ernie's hand and started toward home. Just as he left the schoolyard, he heard himself say, "When we get home, I'm going to take a belt to your bottom like I should have done years ago, boy. You will not show that kind of disrespect to anyone, but most especially your teacher."

He had no clue where the words had come from, but once they were out, he almost smiled. Yes, Ernie needed to be taken in hand. He'd never tell that little spitfire of a teacher he agreed with her, though. No way.

Chapter Three

ANNA WAS NERVOUS ALL through dinner, wondering what Mr. Hanson would say if he heard about her kissing Mr. Hoover. She wanted to kick herself. She still didn't know the man's first name, but she'd replayed that kiss in her mind a dozen times. What was it about him that made her want to kiss him, when she'd thwarted the attentions of several other men in her life?

When nothing happened before bed, she breathed a little more evenly, no longer as worried.

The week went by terribly slowly for her as she watched over her shoulder for someone to come and fire her at any moment. She spent a lot of time trying to figure out whose pink skirt she'd seen Monday afternoon, but she had no idea. Was it a small child who would tell her parents? Was it an older girl who would come to her? She had no idea. What would she do if she couldn't hold down the job? Mr. Hanson would have no problem kicking her out of his house into the street.

She could always try to marry, but every time she met a man she was paralyzed with fear. Well, every time she met one except Mr. Hoover. What had come over her anyway? She still couldn't figure out why she'd kissed the man as she had.

Ernie was better behaved than he had been, seeming to think before he acted out in class, which thrilled Anna. Maybe his father had realized how ridiculous he was being and decided to talk to him after all.

She was feeling much better about her position by the time Saturday morning rolled around. If no one had said anything yet, surely they wouldn't. She was in her room grading papers when there was a loud knock on her door.

"Miss Simmons, you need to come into the parlor right now!" Mr. Hanson's voice sounded even angrier than it usually did.

Anna's eyes widened. Was this it? Had whoever had seen them finally told what they'd seen? She jumped up from her chair at the vanity she was using as a desk and hurriedly fixed her hair, before walking into the parlor. She forced herself to take deep breaths the whole way, worried that she would embarrass herself.

When she arrived, she saw one of her students, Susie, who was only six standing in front of a man who was seated on the sofa. He was a big bear of a man and Anna wanted to hide behind the piano.

Mr. Hanson captured her attention then, speaking in a softer, kinder voice than she'd ever heard from him. "Susie, why don't you tell us all what you saw on Monday afternoon?"

Anna's heart sank. This was it. She was about to be fired, and she had no idea what she would do when that happened.

Susie looked at Anna, her eyes filled with tears, and she told her story, her lisp more pronounced than usual. "I thaw thum pretty flowerth on my way home from thchool, and I thought they were tho pretty, that I wanted to take thum to Mith Thimmonth. I picked a whole bouquet. When I got back to the thchool, I thaw Mith Thimmonth kithing a man I'd never theen before, right there in the clathroom." She was crying loudly by the end of her little speech. "I'm thorry, Mith Thimmonth!"

Anna smiled kindly at the little girl. "You have nothing to be sorry for, Susie." And she didn't. Anna was the one who'd made a mistake, not the sweet little girl with the blond pigtails standing in front of her.

"What do you have to say for yourself, Miss Simmons?" Mr. Hanson's voice was as mean as she'd ever heard it once it was directed on her.

Anna straightened her back. "I don't know what I can say. A man grabbed me and kissed me, and Susie happened along just then." She didn't add that she'd enjoyed the kiss, but she didn't think that Mr.

Hanson really cared what had happened anyway. He wanted to punish her, and he would.

Mr. Hanson took a deep breath. "So you're trying to tell me a man you'd never met walked into the schoolhouse and grabbed you and kissed you without you inviting him to?"

Anna thought carefully about his words, not wanting to lie. "Yes, that's exactly what I'm telling you."

Mr. Hanson glared at her. "You are dismissed from your position, Miss Simmons. You have until the sundown tonight to retrieve your belongings from my home and to get anything you may have left at the schoolhouse. Good day." He turned and left the room then, obviously not caring that he left a little girl and her father as well as Anna in the room.

Susie was sobbing by that point, seemingly over guilt at having told what she'd seen. Anna knew her first priority needed to be to the child. She dropped to one knee and opened her arms, and Susie flew into them. "I'm tho thorry, Mith Thimmonth!"

"I know, Susie. I know. No one is angry with you." Anna realized as soon as the words were out of her mouth that they were true. She wasn't angry with Susie. She was angry with Mr. Hoover for kissing her in the first place, because she hadn't asked to be kissed, but she wasn't mad at Susie.

When Susie had quieted, Anna stood up. She looked at Susie's father, who had been quiet through everything that happened. "I'm terribly sorry this happened, Mr. Johnston."

Mr. Johnston shook his head sadly. "All I really wanted was for him to tell you it was inappropriate for you to be kissing in the schoolroom where any of the children could walk in on you. I had no idea he'd fire you."

Anna smiled ruefully. "I knew as soon as I realized someone had seen me that this would be the result if it came to Mr. Hanson's attention." She shrugged. "I guess I need to figure out what to do next."

She had some money saved, but not nearly enough. "Is there a boarding house in town by any chance?"

"No, ma'am. Wiggieville doesn't have anything as fancy as that."

"I was afraid you'd say that." She rubbed the back of her neck. "I think I'll walk over to the mercantile and see if there are any job postings there." They followed her to the door. "I look forward to seeing you at church tomorrow," she told Susie.

Susie smiled at her, putting her hand in hers. "I'm glad you're not mad at me."

"Why would I be angry with you? You did nothing wrong," Anna said.

Anna watched the two walk off down the street toward the farm Anna knew they had just outside of town. She walked the other way down the street toward the mercantile. Surely there was some type of bulletin board there like there was back in Beckham.

She entered the store and waved to the owner of the mercantile, Mr. Stemmons. She'd seen him at church several times, so she felt as if she knew him. She walked to the back of the store where he was working. "Do you have a 'help wanted' bulletin board here?" Her voice was soft, as it always was when talking to someone she didn't know well, but she was proud that she was able to get the words out.

"Well, I have one, but it's just for people looking for cowboys and such. You lookin' for work?" He eyed her skeptically, obviously wondering why the teacher would be looking for work in the middle of the school year.

She blushed, nodding. She didn't want to admit she'd been fired, but she knew it would be all over town any minute. "I am. Do you know of anyone?"

He nodded. "Actually, I do. There was someone in town lookin' for a housekeeper just the other day."

"Do you know where it was?" She didn't want to get too excited about the prospect, because someone could have been hired, but the idea of working there was more than she'd had an hour ago.

"Sure. They live out at the old Kyle Ranch. Just take the road headin' west, and walk for about a mile. It'll be the first house you come to once you're out of town on the left side of the road."

Anna nodded, happy that there was at least a possibility of her getting a job. She needed to have something lined up before the end of the day. She knew she could always go begging to Julia again, but she didn't want to do that. She'd rather find something without her friend's help.

"Thank you, Mr. Stemmons."

"Anytime." He watched her leave his store and walk toward the west with a bemused look on his face. If he were twenty years younger, and unmarried, he'd be chasing after her himself. Why didn't she just pick a man and marry him?

Anna looked around her at the now green grass as she walked toward the old Kyle Ranch. When she'd first arrived, everything had been brown from drought. It was amazing what a transformation a few weeks could make.

She enjoyed her walk, even though she was fretting about a new job, because she had time to think. She was glad she wouldn't have to deal with Mr. Hoover any longer. Her experiences with him had been more than she could handle anyway.

When she got to the ranch, she saw a cowboy, getting off of his horse and putting it into the stable. She walked up to him, barely able to raise her face to mumble, "Is the owner of the ranch around?"

The cowboy nodded. "Out behind the house fixin' fences. You want me to take you to him?"

"Yes, please," she whispered. She hated being around men she didn't know. Mr. Stemmons was easy, because she'd talked to him frequently at church, and he'd always been kind to her, but this man made her feel almost paralyzed with fear.

The man nodded, studying her closely. "You got business with him?"

She nodded. "I'm inquiring about the housekeeper position."

"Oh! Yeah, he needs a housekeeper bad." He started walking in the direction of the house, and she followed along behind him.

"How long you been in Wiggieville?" he asked, obviously trying to put her at ease.

"Just a month."

"A month? How come I ain't metcha yet?"

"I've been teaching here. Do you go to church? I've been there every Sunday."

"You're the teacher? I've heard some...stories about you." The man sounded like he was trying to withhold a laugh.

She wasn't about to ask. He stopped walking, and she looked up, noticing immediately a man with dark hair and broad shoulders bent over a fence with a tool in his hand. She did notice his bottom as well, but she didn't mean to. He was a very sexy looking man.

"Hey, boss? There's a lady here, wantin' to talk about bein' a housekeeper for ya."

Jesse smiled. He had given up on the idea of hiring a woman to cook and clean for him, and he knew that he was desperate. Why, he'd even thought of sending off for a mail order bride, just so he'd have someone to cook and clean for him. He turned, the smile fading from his lips when he saw Miss Simmons standing in front of him. "What are you doing here?" He didn't want to even talk to her, especially if there was a woman there willing to be his housekeeper.

Anna frowned. "I could ask you the same thing!" She folded her arms over her chest. "I can't work for you! You're not married, and it wouldn't be proper at all." Why hadn't she thought to ask the name of the man needing a housekeeper before she'd walked all the way from town.

"Why would I hire a little spitfire like you? I need someone who knows how to cook and clean, not a little hoity-toity school teacher." He looked her up and down as if he didn't think she had any idea how to work.

"I know how to cook and clean. I'm very good at it actually. I just can't work for an unmarried man. It wouldn't be proper. Even if he *is* the one who got me fired from my job."

He grinned, looking like he was trying not to laugh. "How'd I get you fired? I didn't do anything." Why would she blame him for whatever had gotten her fired? From what he'd seen she was always flying off the handle about something. How could it be his fault?

She was so angry with him, she couldn't see straight. She forgot all about having an audience and walked closer to him until she was all but standing on his feet. "You're the one who grabbed me and kissed me in the schoolhouse. Did you forget we were seen?"

His eyes widened. He had forgotten. She was without a job and it *was* his fault. "Well, you shouldn't have let me kiss you then, should you?" He was just being belligerent by saying the words, knowing he was going to have to help her find a solution.

She was so angry she couldn't contain it another minute. She kicked him. She'd never done anything violent in her life, but she kicked him as hard as she could, and it felt so good, she did it again. "I hate you! You come here with your disobedient, out-of-control child, walk into my school and kiss me, getting me fired. Now I'm in a strange place, where I know no one! What am I supposed to do? You've cost me my job and lost me my place to live!"

He looked at her, feeling more attracted to her than he had to any woman since Deborah's death. "I can't hire you. You're right, it wouldn't be proper." He looked over and realized one of his cowboys was watching their exchange. He waved him away. "Get out of here. This is private!"

Anna took an immediate step back. "You're not going to try to kiss me again are you?" Her heart was already beating faster, just at the idea. She hated herself for liking the idea as much as she did.

He shook his head, but waited for the cowboy to get out of range. "Look, I do feel responsible for you losing your job. I can't hire you, because people would talk." He took a deep breath, wondering if he was doing the right thing, but having no idea what else he could possibly do. "How 'bout marrying me instead?"

She stared at him in shock. Had he really just offered to marry her? They'd only met once before. "I...I don't know how to even answer that, Mr. Hoover. You're a stranger to me." A stranger that she enjoyed kissing.

"I'm not asking you to share my bed. It would be a business arrangement. I'm not ready for a real wife, but I do need someone who can cook and clean for me, and I need help with Ernie. You'd do everything a wife does except share a room with me. The house is big. There are plenty of bedrooms. You'd just pick one and it would be yours."

"So you're asking me to be your housekeeper, and help you raise your son, but with the cloak of marriage to protect my reputation?" It truly wasn't a bad idea if they could keep from killing one another...and keep their hands off each other, of course.

He nodded. "Yeah, that's pretty much it."

She thought about it for a moment. It's pretty much what she'd thought she'd be getting with Tom, but she wouldn't have to share his bed. "What happens if one of us falls in love with someone else?"

He shrugged. "I have no idea what we'd do then. I really don't. We'll both have to try not to let that happen, and if it does, we'll cross that bridge when we come to it." He knew he wasn't endearing himself to her with his answer, but he didn't know what else to tell her.

She sighed. She wanted to know she'd have security, but this sounded like the best offer she'd get. Being a wife without the bedroom duties sounded wonderful to her. She stepped toward him and held out her right hand to shake. "I'll do it."

He grinned, happy with her agreement. He didn't realize he'd been holding his breath until she agreed. His hand swallowed hers as he shook it. He felt a rush of electricity shoot through him as soon as he touched her, but he ignored it. He didn't have feelings like that for women any longer. He'd married Deborah, and he'd promised to be true to her. He would still be true to her. "I guess we could get married next Saturday?" he suggested.

She frowned. "I have to have everything cleared out of the house where I live today. I've not only lost my job, but I've lost my home."

He shrugged. "Well, let's hope the preacher is around to marry us then." He strode toward the house, planning on finding Ernie and heading into town. It was the only right thing to do after all.

Chapter Four

ANNA FOLLOWED ALONG behind Mr. Hoover, not certain where he was going, but refusing to go into the house with him, because it wouldn't be proper with them both being unmarried and no chaperone around. She stayed on the front porch, sitting in a porch swing that was there. She knew it must be from the previous owners because Mr. Hoover didn't seem like the porch swing type to her at all.

A porch swing was more of a finishing touch on a house than something a man would do. It was comfortable though, and she liked the idea of doing some mending on the porch when it was cool outside. It was October, and she still found the weather much too hot for her tastes. Didn't it ever cool off in Texas?

She frowned. She still didn't know the man's first name. He'd kissed her, and she was about to marry him, but she didn't know his name? What was wrong with her?

He came out of the house a moment later with Ernie in tow. Ernie glared at her. "You're not my mother!"

She stood up, looking at the boy. "I never said I was, but I will do my best to feed you and make sure you wear proper clothes and act right." What else could she say? She knew he didn't want a new mother, but she was stepping into that role, and he was going to respect her.

Ernie was obviously upset at the prospect of her marrying his father, but he said nothing more, just looking down at his feet.

Mr. Hoover looked at her. "You ready? Let's get this over with." He gestured to the swing. "Wait here while I hitch up the horses."

Jesse strode off to the stable, wondering if he could possibly be doing the right thing. He needed to get some help with his son, but was marrying the right way to do it? And he was attracted to her, whether he wanted to be or not. He didn't need her to constantly be around. What was he thinking marrying again anyway? And her? She was the last woman he should marry.

He took a deep breath to calm himself, realizing Ernie was standing there looking at him. "Son, I'm not marrying her because I love her. I made her lose her job. I'm giving her another one." He wasn't certain if the words were for her benefit, his, or Ernie's.

Ernie nodded solemnly. "But, you still only love Ma, right?"

Jesse nodded emphatically. "I still only love your ma." He made quick work of hitching up the team and drove to the house.

He drove what was obviously his farm wagon, but she didn't ask if he had a buggy. She needed this marriage to be respectable but still have a place to live and work to do. She knew better than to antagonize him at that point. She climbed into the wagon without help, because he didn't offer any, and sat as far from him on the seat as the buckboard allowed.

They didn't speak as they drove into town, stopping in front of a small house. The three of them went to the door, and it was answered by a short middle-aged man with silver streaking his brown hair and dancing blue eyes. He smiled at Anna. "Miss Simmons! I wasn't aware you were acquainted with Mr. Hoover."

Anna bit back the 'unfortunately' that danced on the tip of her tongue. She was surprised to know that Mr. Hoover had taken the time to get to introduce himself to the preacher. He didn't seem the type to care much about his spiritual health. "Yes, we want to be married."

The preacher nodded solemnly. "Of course." He took their wanting to marry in stride. "Come right in."

Anna followed him into the house, knowing the other two would follow quickly behind. "Thank you for taking your time to see us today." She didn't expect Mr. Hoover to be polite, so she thought she should be to make up for him.

The pastor turned around in the center of the room and looked at them both. "I'm afraid you're both new enough in town that I only know your last names." He looked at Anna. "Your Christian name is?"

"Anna," she whispered. She wished he would hurry and just get it over with. As a child she'd dreamed of what her wedding would be like, as most girls did, and this was not it. She wanted it over and done with so she could get away from people and just cry.

"I'm Jesse," Mr. Hoover said, his voice deep and strong.

The pastor nodded. "All right. If you will join hands."

Anna froze for a moment before offering her hand to Jesse. She had to learn to think of him as Jesse and not Mr. Hoover. He would be her husband; she couldn't refer to him formally forever.

The ceremony was short and sweet. When he pronounced them man and wife and told Jesse to kiss his bride, Anna felt a moment of panic. She turned to him, raising her lips to his, her eyes searching his face. He leaned down and brushed a quick soft kiss just beside her lips, not touching hers with his own. What was wrong with him? She was fine to kiss when she was some random stranger in the schoolhouse, but when she was his wife, he couldn't kiss her? What kind of man had she married?

Jesse straightened up, nodding his thanks to the reverend. "Thank you, Pastor. We appreciate your time." He took Ernie's hand and headed for the door, leaving Anna to trail behind them in his wake.

Anna looked at the preacher for a moment, befuddled, before she half-ran after the Hoovers. "We have to stop at the Hansons' house to get my things," she reminded him. Mr. Hoover was the type to burn all her things if she hadn't picked them up by the time he'd specified.

"You'll have to tell me where that is. I'm afraid I know where the church is, the mercantile, and the pastor's house. Everything else I need directions to." He hated to admit not knowing where something was, but he was new enough in town that he figured she'd understand. In another month, the excuse wouldn't be good enough, and he'd have to know how to do everything.

She directed him the short distance down the street to Mr. Hanson's house, before jumping down. "I'll be right back." She was surprised when Jesse jumped down as well.

"I'll get your things for you." He followed behind her, leaving Ernie in the wagon as they stepped inside the house.

"Mrs. Hanson?" she called. "I'm here to get my things." She didn't want the older woman to be frightened if she was home alone. She genuinely liked Mrs. Hanson and wished she knew how to get her out of her marriage, but Mrs. Hanson seemed happy enough.

Mr. Hanson came out of his study and glared at her and Jesse. "So is this the man you were whoring with in the schoolhouse?" he asked. His face was flushed with his anger, and he stood with his hands on his hips as if daring her to deny it.

Anna blushed, rushing to her room and ignoring him. She was so thankful not to have to live under the odious old man's roof any longer. She heard. "Well? Are you the one she was kissing?" The word *kissing* sounded like a cardinal sin coming out of Mr. Hanson's mouth.

"Yes, I am. She's a beautiful girl. You can't blame me for kissing her." Jesse looked Mr. Hanson up and down. "I'm sure you've kissed at least one pretty girl in your life." He wasn't about to let the man insult his wife, whether he had feelings for her or not.

"I can and I will. I can't believe you had the gall to try and kiss her right there in the schoolhouse."

"I can't believe you'd fire a woman and turn her out into the street before hearing the entire story. I kissed *her* in the schoolhouse. She had nothing to do with it." Jesse wasn't worried about the half truth, because he knew Anna would never have initiated the kiss. She hadn't fought him off, though. He knew for a fact she'd enjoyed it just as much as he had. He forced his mind to stop thinking about that kiss. Now that she was his wife, it seemed to be all he could think about. How soft she'd been in his arms when he'd held her. How sweet her lips had been beneath his own.

"She should have had the morals to slap your face and walk away. Instead, she let you kiss her. She has no right to be a moral guide for the children in our community."

Jesse snorted. "You're an old bigot. I'm glad she's got somewhere better to go now." He'd never met anyone he'd disliked on first meeting quite as much as he did Mr. Hanson. Burying a fist in his face seemed like a wonderful idea just then, but he didn't want to upset Anna more than this visit already would.

"Did you marry the jezebel?"

"Yes, I did, and if I ever hear you talk about my wife that way again, I will personally hunt you down like the weasel you are." He strode off in the direction Anna had disappeared to and stuck his head in the only open door. "You ready, sweetheart?"

Anna's eyes danced as they met his. "Sweetheart?" she mouthed. At his shrug, she pointed to her trunk and picked up her carpet bag. "It's right there, darling." She'd heard the entire exchange between the two men and couldn't believe Jesse had come so readily to her defense.

He raised an eyebrow but said nothing as he hefted her trunk over one shoulder and led the way out of the house, hoping she'd follow closely behind him and not say anything else to that odious man.

Anna stopped at the door. "I hope you find a new teacher quickly."

Mr. Hanson stood sputtering for a moment before yelling after her, "I will. And her last name won't be Simmons!"

Anna ignored him as Jesse put his hands at her waist, and gently lifted her into the wagon, carefully tucking her skirts around her like he was infatuated with her. As soon as they were away from the house, she looked at him. "Thank you for standing up for me."

He nodded. "I may not be in love with you, but you're still my wife, and no man needs to be talking badly about you." He gave her a funny look. "What did he mean by the next teacher not being named 'Simmons?'"

She laughed softly. "This is a crazy story, but the woman who came out here to teach and ended up married to my fiancé had the same last name as me. That's how the confusion happened."

He shook his head. "That's crazy."

She smiled as she looked out the other side of the wagon. He may not know it yet, but he was going to make her a very good husband.

They drove home in silence, and when they reached the ranch, he carried her trunk inside, leaving her to get down herself. "I'll be back at five for supper. Have it waiting for me." He walked off without looking back even once. So that was how it was going to be. He'd do his job, and she'd do hers, and they would have as little contact as possible. She could handle that.

Anna watched him go, her stomach growling loudly to remind her she hadn't even had lunch yet. She looked down at Ernie who didn't look at all pleased to have her in his home. "Did you eat lunch? I'm hungry!"

Ernie shook his head. "No. You came around lunch time." He eyed her warily, as if he wasn't certain what to think of her being in his house.

"I did, didn't I?" She walked toward the large kitchen at the back of the big ranch house. "Let's see what we can find to eat that doesn't need to be cooked for hours."

She ended up making them each a bacon sandwich on toast, while she cleaned the kitchen, which looked as if it hadn't been cleaned in the two weeks the Hoovers had been in Texas. Once she was done, she located a pork roast in the cellar, which she put into the oven and she peeled carrots and potatoes to go with it. Ernie sat at the table the whole time, eating his sandwich and watching her, as if he were worried she'd do something wrong. She had no doubt that he would run to his father if she did something that he didn't think was right.

When she had dinner in the oven, she turned to the table and shooed Ernie off so she could give it a good cleaning. She then grabbed a broom and swept the floors before getting down on her hands and knees and scrubbing them. She had woken up that morning a single teacher with no prospects, and here she was now, cleaning her kitchen, a wife and a mother. Life was odd in how it threw things at her.

When Jesse got home at the end of his day, he stopped at the well to splash water over his hands and face, something he hadn't done after work since his wife died. He'd always cleaned up for her before going into supper, and he felt he should afford his new wife the same courtesy, whether he wanted to or not. As his wife she deserved his respect, even though he'd never be able to love her.

When he stepped in the back door, the smell of the meat roasting brought a smile to his face. His stomach let out a loud growl, reminding him that he'd skipped lunch again. He walked into the kitchen and stopped in surprise. Everything was sparkling. It looked like even the stove had been blacked. How on earth had that tiny woman done so much work so quickly?

The table was set, and she was standing at the stove stirring something. "I'm just finishing up the gravy. Go ahead and sit down and serve yourself, and by the time you're done, I'll have the gravy on the table."

Jesse collapsed into the chair at the head of the table and sniffed appreciatively. "Dinner smells good."

Anna turned from the counter and smiled. "It should taste good, too. I'm a good cook." She poured the gravy into a bowl and set it on the table. "Let me call Ernie, and then we'll be ready to eat." Her cooking was one thing she had a great deal of confidence in, and she was happy to be able to say she did it well.

Ernie was still obviously upset as he walked into the kitchen, his eyes downcast. He took his spot at the side of the table and fixed his plate. Anna waited until both men had fixed their plates before fixing her own. "I thought you must like pork roast, because I saw some in the cellar," she said.

Jesse nodded. "I've been trying to figure out how to cook one. I've had to throw three away just this week. It'll be nice to have someone around to do the cooking." Whatever he thought of her, whatever else she did, he was thrilled to have a woman who could cook in the house.

Anna looked between the two males. "Who cooked for you back East?"

Jesse shrugged. "After Deborah died, I hired a housekeeper, and she did all the cooking and cleaning." He didn't add that she had been ready to quit when they decided to move, because Ernie had been so out of control.

Anna sighed. "So I'm not taking your wife's place, I'm taking the housekeeper's place." She watched Ernie out of the corner of her eye as she said the words. "I understand." She was hoping that hearing those words would make Ernie feel better about her being there.

Ernie perked up. "That's right. You're just taking old Mrs. Jenkins's place. Not Ma's." He gave her a look that told her it made him feel superior to say so, but she didn't mind at all. She was happy he'd understood what she was trying to say.

Jesse raised an eyebrow at Ernie. "You'll treat her with the same respect you treated your ma with, though. Won't you?" He understood Anna's purpose in the words, but he needed to know his son would be respectful.

Ernie nodded reluctantly. "Yes, Pa." He looked back down at his plate, but he didn't seem nearly as upset as he had earlier.

"Are you going to pray for us?" Anna asked, looking at Jesse.

He nodded, and they all bowed their heads for his simple prayer. As soon as he'd finished, he stuck his fork into the pork roast and took a huge bite. He almost moaned with pleasure. His new wife really could cook. In fact, he'd never had a woman cook so well in his life. "This is good."

She smiled. "I cooked a lot in the orphanage. It was one of my favorite chores." She'd always begged the other girls to trade with her when they were on cooking duty.

"Orphanage? You were raised in an orphanage?" Jesse asked with surprise.

She nodded. "My pa died in the last battle of the War Between the States, but I was already on the way. My ma died of a fever a few weeks after I was born. There weren't any relatives who could take me in, so a neighbor found me and dropped me at the orphanage."

"Where was that? Here in Texas?" he asked. Her accent didn't seem quite right for Texas.

She shook her head. "No, I was raised in Beckham, Massachusetts. I've only been here two weeks longer than you two have." It was strange to realize she was married to a man who knew so little about her, but the circumstances were odd all around.

Jesse stared at her for a moment. "You came out here to teach?" he asked.

"No, I came out here to be a mail order bride." She took a sip of water, before continuing. "I'm terribly shy, and I was nervous about coming here, so I sent a telegram to the man I was supposed to marry and told him I'd be two weeks late. I wanted more time to get ready. The woman who was coming here to teach school had the same last name as me, and she arrived on the stage I was supposed to be on. Somehow, she ended up married to my groom, and when I got here, he was married, but the town needed a teacher." Her eyes met his for the first time since she'd started her story. "I hate teaching, but I'd done it back East, so I was qualified. It was better to take her position as a teacher than try to find something else." She didn't add that she'd been petrified that she would have nowhere to go once she arrived in town and realized what had happened.

"That's crazy. Why didn't she tell him that she was the teacher and not his bride?"

Anna shrugged. "She said she kept trying to tell him, and he kept kissing her, and it muddled her brain." She hadn't understood that when Julia had first told the story, but she certainly did now. After kissing Jesse in the schoolhouse that day, she understood what it meant to have a truly muddled mind.

Jesse shook his head. "Did they even apologize?"

"Yes, they did. It was an honest mistake, and really, I found Tom to be very intimidating. I don't think I'd have been able to marry him anyway. I'm extremely shy."

"You don't seem at all shy to me," he told her.

She blushed. "Well, you made me angry from the first moment we met. I was more of a fishwife with you than I've ever been with a man."

"I can understand that." He looked down at Ernie for a moment, wishing he knew how to explain how much his son had changed since his mother died. "We're all going to church in the morning. We go every Sunday. I'll work when we get home, though. I have a lot that needs to be done to get the ranch in shape. I purchased it sight unseen from an older couple, and the man hadn't really kept things up in a couple of years. I'd like it to be how I want it before winter rolls around."

She nodded. "I won't say anything about you breaking the Sabbath. I understand things like that need to happen sometimes." She sighed. "I'll probably try to get some laundry and mending done tomorrow as well. It looks like there's a lot that's been neglected since you arrived." Anna's words sounded like a complaint, but her tone of voice didn't. She truly didn't mind the work, because she was glad to have it.

He nodded. "And we spent months on the trail before we got here. There are a lot of clothes that need to be mended." He nodded at Ernie. "He's outgrown almost everything he owns. He's going to need new clothes. I don't think his pants can be taken down any more."

"I enjoy sewing. It will give me something to do while he's in school." Anna smiled at Ernie, hoping he'd smile back, but he didn't. He just continued to stare through her.

"I hate school," Ernie moaned.

"I don't blame you, but school is good for you. It will help you learn to get along with others, and you can learn how to ranch on the weekends. Do you want to be a rancher like your pa someday?" She knew he did, and she was ready with an answer if he said 'yes.'

Ernie nodded emphatically. "I do. It's all I've ever wanted. I think I'll be a really good rancher. I should be able to stay home with him all day to learn how to ranch instead of sitting in a schoolroom learning stupid things I don't need to know."

"Well, don't you think there are things you can learn in school that will help you to be a better rancher? When your pa is offered money for his herd, don't you think he has to use arithmetic to decide if it's a good deal or not? What about reading? What if there's a new feed to give cattle that will make them grow up bigger and stronger? Should he keep up with that so he can keep up with the rest of his industry? I think he should."

Ernie thought about it for a moment. "Well, yes."

"He has to be able to read well and do arithmetic to make that work. So you need to learn both of those things, don't you?"

Ernie sighed. "You tricked me."

Anna smiled. "I didn't trick you. I reasoned with you. They're two different things."

He played with his food for a moment before taking his first bite. He'd obviously been reluctant to eat it, because she'd cooked it and his father had liked it. After the first bite, he ate quickly, washing it all down with water as fast as he could. When he'd cleaned his plate, he jumped to his feet. "May I be excused?"

Jesse nodded, watching as his son ran from the room. "He's trying really hard not to like you."

"I can see that. I wish I could convince him that I'm not out to replace his mother. I know he had a good mother, and that he loved her. I don't need to be that mother." She almost felt sorry for the boy, knowing he missed his mother as much as he did.

"What do you hope to get out of this marriage?" Jesse asked suddenly, watching her face.

She blinked a few times. "What do you mean?"

"Well, most women want children from marriage, but you won't get them from ours. Some want security. I don't think you'll feel that from this marriage. What exactly do you think you're going to get from it?" He knew his words were cold, but he needed to be certain she had no expectations other than what he was willing to offer her.

Anna shrugged, looking down at her plate. "When I came out here as a mail order bride, I was more than happy to marry the man waiting for me. I planned to be a good cook, and clean to the best of my ability. I feel like I'm very qualified to keep a home and do everything that's entailed with being a housekeeper, even with taking care of children. The only thing I was really worried about was the marriage bed." Her eyes met his. "You've made it clear that you don't expect that from me, so to me, it sounds like the perfect marriage. It sounds like exactly what I want and need from you." She was very happy with the situation, even though it was an odd one.

He fixed himself another plate of food as he thought over her answer. "You really don't want that part of marriage? You don't want children?"

She shrugged. "Of course, I'd like children of my own, but it doesn't hurt me not to have them. I'm going to be a step-mother to Ernie, so my maternal feelings will have an outlet of sorts. I'm glad I don't have to share your bed to fulfill that."

He was surprised by her answer. "My first wife wanted nothing more than to have babies. She loved the marriage bed."

Anna blushed. "I don't think you should be telling me that, do you?" She stood up and started clearing the table, taking the water she'd started heating earlier and pouring it into the basin. She started to take away the platter with what was left of the roast on it, so she could store it away, and they could eat it for lunch the following day, but he caught her wrist.

"Leave it. I'll eat most of it before I'm done. I burn a lot of energy during the day, and I missed lunch today." He watched her work while he finished eating, and most of the roast was gone before he was done. He polished off all the potatoes and most of the carrots as well.

She sighed when she saw what little was left. He was going to take a lot of energy for her to feed. There went her planned lunch for the following day.

Once the dishes were done and the small amount of food left was put away, she climbed the stairs to get ready for bed. Ernie was sitting at the top of the stairs waiting for her. "I don't want to live with my teacher."

She sat down beside him on the top step, thinking hard about the best way to respond to him. "You know I'm not your teacher anymore, right? There is no teacher at the school for a while. They're looking for another one." She didn't want to come right out and tell him she'd been fired, but she needed him to understand she would no longer be teaching him.

"No teacher?" He perked up at her words. "I don't have to go to school?"

"Not until they find a new one, I guess. Do you think while you have a break from school, you can try to get used to me? I'd really like to see you act like the good boy I know you are inside, instead of showing me the kid that everyone sees. You know which one I mean. The one who's always trying to get attention and acting out in school. That boy isn't who I'm looking for. I'm looking for the boy inside you who obeys his father and does his chores when he's asked. Can you show him to me?"

Ernie shrugged, acting as if he didn't know what she was talking about, but she thought she may have gotten through to him. She stood up and walked to her room, closing the door with a snap behind her. She carefully unpacked her clothes, and hung them in the wardrobe before making up her bed with the sheets that had been thrown at the foot of it for her use. She would get everything cleaned upstairs soon, she promised herself. It was filthy, and no one should have to live that way.

As she closed her eyes for the night, she said a silent prayer of thanks that things had worked out how they did. Jesse could be an overbearing donkey, but she was certain she would settle in nicely. She fell asleep with a smile on her lips. Life would be good in the Hoover household. She was certain of it.

Chapter Five

ANNA FELT UNCOMFORTABLE as she walked into church the following morning, knowing rumors of her getting fired must be flying around the small town. She sat with her new family, Ernie between her and Jesse, and paid rapt attention to the sermon.

As soon as the service was over, Julia rushed over and grabbed Anna's arm. "We have got to talk!"

Anna followed Julia to a corner of the church and all but cried on her friends shoulder. "I guess you heard?"

"I heard you were fired! How many teachers is this town going to go through in a year?" Julia shook her head, obviously not blaming Anna for what had happened.

Anna shrugged. "I hated Mr. Hanson the day I met him and he was so rude to you. He seems a hundred times worse to me now."

"So what happened? Why did he fire you, and why are you sitting with the new family?"

Anna took a deep breath. "Ernie was a new student two weeks ago. He was a monster. At the end of his first week at school, I sent a letter asking his father to meet me after school on Monday so we could discuss his behavior. He met me, and we fought. He actually allowed Ernie to stick his tongue out at me in front of him, and never said a word to stop him." She knew Julia would feel the same way about Ernie's disrespectful behavior that she did.

Julia's eyes widened. "How rude!"

"Yes, and then he grabbed me and kissed me."

Julia blinked a few times as if she hadn't understood what her friend had said. "He grabbed you and kissed you? Just right there in the schoolhouse? In front of Ernie?"

"I sent Ernie out to play on the playground as soon as Mr. Hoover got there. Yes, he just grabbed me and kissed me. At first, I tried to push him away, but..." She trailed off, looking around to see if anyone was listening to her. "I liked it." She was embarrassed to admit it, but if anyone could understand enjoying kissing a stranger, then it was Julia.

Julia covered her hand with her mouth, and at first Anna thought she was shocked, but then she realized her friend was trying not to laugh. "It's not funny! I guess it's kind of what happened with you and Tom, isn't it?"

"Well, except Tom was kissing me in the middle of the street, and he thought I was his fiancé. You and Mr. Hoover were just standing in the middle of the schoolroom kissing." Julia frowned. "So how did you end up fired?"

Anna sighed. "Susie saw us kissing, and she told her father. Her father assumed that Mr. Hanson would have a talk with me, so no more unsuspecting students would walk in on their teacher kissing a man in the schoolhouse." She shook her head. "You know Mr. Hanson as well as I do. He didn't just talk to me. He fired me on the spot and told me that I had to be out of his house by nightfall."

"You could have come to me, you know."

"Oh, I know, but you're a newlywed. I didn't want to interrupt your honeymoon again. So I went to the mercantile and asked if there were any jobs for women around. Mr. Stemmons knew of someone looking for a housekeeper, and he gave me directions. I walked out to the house he told me to go to, and it was the Hoover Ranch."

Julia gasped, putting her hand over her mouth. "You're not working for him now, are you? Your reputation will be ruined if you're living with a widower and his son!"

Anna shook her head. "No, he offered me a job, but I refused, because I couldn't do it. I told him he was the reason I was fired, so he offered to marry me, but..." She leaned really close to make certain no one would hear. She knew it wasn't proper to talk about some things, especially in church, but she had to talk to her friend and get her opinion. "We're not sharing a marriage bed. I have a room of my own."

Julia made a face. "But you kissed in the schoolhouse, and you both liked it?"

Anna blushed. "Well, I liked it, but I don't know if he did."

Julia frowned. "I'm certain he did. It's not going to last."

"The marriage? I hope it does, because I don't want to be without a place to go again anytime soon."

"No, the not sharing a marriage bed. You'll both break down." Julia sounded certain, but how could she know?

Anna shook her head. "That's the only part I was afraid of when I came out here to marry Tom. I'm glad it's this way."

Julia laughed. "You're glad now, but that won't last either. You two will both want things to be different soon. You can't live together and not touch each other. It's just not natural."

Anna shrugged. "It's what we both want."

"Can I ask you something?" Julia asked.

Anna eyed her skeptically, half afraid of what was on her friend's mind. "What's that?"

"Why did you let him kiss you when you don't seem to like him?"

Anna bit her lip, wondering just how much she should admit. "Well, he...he was angry with me, and he grabbed me and kissed me. I really didn't have a choice in the matter."

"He kissed you in anger?" Julia frowned. "Tom's never kissed me in anger. That must have been odd."

Anna shrugged. "I don't know. It's the only time I've ever been kissed except the wedding kiss, and that kiss wasn't even on my lips."

Julia sighed. "Well, you'll understand what I mean soon then." She shrugged. "Bright side of it all is that we live less than a mile apart now. We can meet in the middle and have picnics. Or better yet, you can come over for tea or coffee, or I can go to your house for tea or coffee."

Anna smiled at the idea. "I like that thought. Of course, I need to do a lot of cleaning before I can have anyone over for any reason. I don't know how they could have made such a big mess in just two weeks of living there. The place looks like it hasn't been really scrubbed in years." It was a good thing she didn't mind hard work.

"It's a possibility. I know that Mrs. Kyle was older, and she'd had a stroke. She may not have been able to clean at all their last couple of years there. That's why they went back East. Their daughter lives out there, and they need help."

Anna nodded, understanding finally. "I see. Well, I can whip it into shape in no time. It's just going to take some hard work."

"Would you like me to come over and help you one day this week? I've got plenty of time now that I'm not teaching."

Anna thought about it and finally nodded. "I don't necessarily want the help, but I'd love the company. Why don't you come out Tuesday after lunch, and we'll have tea, and I may put you to work."

"You will put me to work, you mean?"

Anna grinned, hugging her friend tightly. "I may put you to work. I can't wait to see you then. Do you know how to get to the ranch?"

Julia nodded. "Of course, I do. I'll be by after I finish up the lunch dishes."

ANNA SPENT THE AFTERNOON washing the clothes and hanging them out to dry. The bedding needed a good washing as well, but there just weren't enough clotheslines to do everything in one day. She'd do the rest on Monday.

She made up a pie for dessert from the blackberries she'd spotted on the side of the road on her way home from church. She and Ernie had taken tin pails and rushed out to pick them as soon as the clothes were on the line. Ernie had been reluctant at first, but when she told him she wanted the berries to make a couple of pies for supper, he'd been more than willing.

They'd talked while they picked the berries. He'd complained again that she would never be his mother, and she'd told him she had no desire to take his mother's place. "My mother died when I was just a few weeks old. I don't even know when my birthday is. I know what month, but that's all."

"You don't know your birthday?" His voice sounded shocked.

She shook her head. "No, because my pa died before I was even born, and my ma died too soon to tell me when my birthday was."

"That's sad."

She shrugged. "So I understand not wanting a new ma. You already had one, and she sounds like she was a pretty wonderful lady. I'm not going to take her place. Instead, I'm going to be someone who helps around the house, and helps guide you the right way, without being a ma. Will that work for you?"

Ernie nodded. "I guess. Can you do that?"

"Of course, I can." They walked home from the berry patch with a new understanding of each other, and he had a new respect for her.

By the time Jesse came home for supper, there was a huge pot of beans with cornbread and the pies for dessert. He walked into the kitchen as if in a trance. "I haven't had food this good since my mother died."

Ernie looked at his father with surprise. "You mean my mother right?"

Jesse's eyes widened, but he nodded. Over the top of his head, Jesse mouthed to Anna, "No, I mean my mother."

Anna stifled a laugh as she put big bowls of beans on the table, along with a plate of cornbread. After the prayer, Jesse talked a bit about his day. "When we moved in here, the fences were in terrible shape. We were always having cows escape. I was able to patch up the worst of the holes quickly, but now I'm going back around to patch the smaller holes. I can't spare my men to work on them, so right now, it's just me. I need to hire on about twice as many men as I currently have as well. I don't know how Kyle was able to make this ranch pay for as long as it did."

"So are you disappointed you bought it from him?" she asked, not knowing much about how ranches worked.

He shook his head, taking a big swallow of water, and pouring himself more from the pitcher on the table. "Really, I'm not upset at all. I've always wanted to be a rancher, and now I am one. This place is a dream come true for me. It's going to be hard work for a lot of years to come, but I'm young. I've got a lot of work left in me."

She looked at him for a moment, and blinked, realizing that she didn't even know how old her husband was. "How old are you?"

He looked at her for a minute, before laughing. "I guess that's something a wife has a right to know about her husband, doesn't she? I'm twenty-eight. I married at nineteen, and we had Ernie when I was twenty. She was seventeen when we married." He eyed her for a moment before asking, "How old are you?"

"I'm twenty. I taught for two years back East and swore I'd never do it again before I moved out here to be a bride."

"I saw you talking to a woman for a while at the back of the church after service this morning. Who was she?"

"That's Julia. She's the one who married Tom, the man I was supposed to marry." Anna knew it sounded strange even as she said the words.

"Are you two friends now?"

Anna nodded emphatically. "She's the best friend I've ever had. I know it's odd, but it's just worked out for us. When I was standing in the middle of town looking around for Tom, who I thought would be waiting for me, she saw me, stopped, and offered me a place to stay until I figured out what I wanted to do."

"Oh, I had no idea she'd helped you so much. No wonder you're friends."

"I stayed with her and Tom for a weekend, and then I moved into the Hansons' house and started teaching."

"Well, you can't hold that against her."

"She's going to come over on Tuesday afternoon after lunch. She thinks she's going to help me finish cleaning the house, but I'm hoping to have it mostly done by then. I might have her help me with some of the mending." She nodded to his shirt. "That shirt has a huge hole in the back of it, and I noticed that you have a seam ripped out of your church shirt as well. I'd like to get those fixed this week."

"That's a lot to do." Mrs. Jenkins had constantly complained about how hard on clothes he was, and she'd rarely been willing to take the time to mend anything.

"It is, but it's all work I enjoy. I want to measure Ernie tomorrow morning and then go into town to get some fabric to start on some new clothes for him. I thought two sets of school clothes and one outfit for church would be good to start with."

Ernie frowned. "I hate new clothes. I hate standing still to be measured."

Anna looked at him with wide eyes. "You do? I know how to make it take just half the time!"

"Really? How?"

"If you stand still the first time, then I won't have to keep redoing it, and it will save a lot of time!"

Ernie made a face. "You like to trick me, don't you?"

Anna smiled. "Not as much as I like for you to do what you're told and stand still." She stood up and walked over to the work table where she had the pies cooling. She picked up one of them and took it to the table, setting it right in the middle. She cut three large slices and put them on saucers, handing them around.

Jesse looked down at the pie with a look of sheer delight. "What kind of pie is this?"

"Blackberry. I saw some on the side of the road on the way home, and Ernie and I picked them. I thought you might like some pie this evening." She watched him to see if he was pleased with her surprise.

"I love pie. You're already spoiling me. I'm not sure that's such a good idea. Next thing you know, I'm going to expect pie for supper every night." Jesse grinned as he took another big bite.

Ernie looked back and forth between them. "Don't start liking each other. It's better when you fight."

Anna looked at Ernie. "You don't want us to get along? You'd rather we fought all the time?"

Ernie seemed to think about that for a moment. "Well, I don't want you to fight so much that you stop cooking good, but I don't want you to like each other too much."

Anna's eyes met Jesse's and she saw that his were twinkling. "He's *your* son."

Jesse reached out and ruffled Ernie's hair. "Yes, he is."

After supper that evening, she sat on the porch swing with her mending and worked on fixing some of the worst holes in his shirts. They both needed new clothes badly, and she would get on that just as soon as she had time. She knew she could get the house finished by Monday evening, even with having to go into town for supplies the next day, and she would start the real sewing on Tuesday. When Julia came over on Tuesday, they could sit and talk while they sewed, which was something she'd always wanted to do.

She wasn't certain why the idea of sewing with a friend appealed to her so much, but the mother of the family she'd lived with in Beckham while she was teaching frequently had friends over in the afternoon, and they would sew together. She would listen to the laughter from her room while she graded papers, desperately wanting to be part of it, but not having the courage to ask.

Jesse came out after a while and interrupted her thoughts, bringing her a lantern. "Can you see well enough to keep working?" he asked.

She shrugged. "Mending holes is easy. It's not going to look great regardless, so how much light I have isn't a big deal."

He sat beside her on the swing, moving the extra clothing items out of his way. "Thanks for working so hard for us. Dinner has been wonderful the past two nights. I had no idea you were such a good cook."

Anna nodded. "I'm glad you've enjoyed it." She stared down at the mending for a moment, not certain what to say to him. It felt so awkward trying to talk to him now that they weren't fighting all the time. "What are your favorite foods?"

He thought about it for a moment. "I like roast a lot. That's why I was trying to learn how to cook it. I like pies and cakes. I have a real sweet tooth. I love to have flapjacks for breakfast, but I have no idea how to make them, so I haven't had them since Deborah died." His face took on a look of sadness after he mentioned his wife.

"You still miss her a lot don't you? Even after three years?" Anna was surprised to see that. The people she knew who had lost spouses had remarried quickly.

He nodded. "I promised her I would never love anyone else. I don't go back on my promises."

She was surprised by his comment. "But even wedding vows say 'til death do us part.' No one expects you to remain faithful after death."

"I expect me to." He couldn't explain it, but he felt like his love with Deborah had been so pure and true, he couldn't imagine settling for anything less.

She felt like his comments gave her no hope for the future at all, and she was certain it should upset her, but it truly didn't. If he couldn't see that she was worth giving up his love for a woman who had been dead for three years, then he wasn't worthy of her anyway. She wasn't certain how she'd handle having no children of her own five years down the road, but she decided she'd try not to borrow trouble. There was enough that found her on a daily basis for her to worry about what would happen in five years.

"You don't think it's in the realm of possibilities that you could meet someone down the road who wouldn't make you forget her, but would make you feel like you could live again?"

"No, I really don't. I have Ernie, and he's all I really need." He stood up and walked toward the back door. "I appreciate all you do, but don't think I'll fall in love with you." The door closed firmly behind him, leaving her alone in the darkness, with only the lantern.

She felt a tear trickle down her cheek. She wasn't in love with him, but she realized she could be. She was married to him, and had given up the right to love anyone else in the world, but he'd let her know in no uncertain terms that he would never love her. Would she be able to live with that? Or would she soon want more from him?

Chapter Six

ANNA WAS UP EARLIER than usual the following morning so she could have breakfast ready for Jesse before he left for work. She'd never really thought about that aspect of being a wife, and realized that she'd really been spoiled by sleeping in as late as she had most mornings that she was teaching. With school starting at nine, she'd slept until half past seven most days, eating what was left from the family's breakfast.

Now that she was a ranch wife, she felt like she needed to be up as soon as the sun was, so she could have breakfast ready before her husband was even awake. She walked outside and collected the eggs before deciding to whip up pancakes and bacon for breakfast.

As she was putting the bacon on the table, Jesse came down the stairs, his hair rumpled from sleep. He was wearing just his work pants, and she blushed, looking down when she saw his bare chest. The people who ran the orphanage where she'd grown up had been extremely careful to keep any sort of nudity behind closed doors. She had never seen a man's bare chest before, and she felt her stomach quickening as she saw her husband's.

With her eyes still averted, she said, "Breakfast will be ready in ten minutes or so. I just need to fry up the pancakes."

He nodded, noticing her discomfort at his bare chest immediately. He pulled the shirt he carried on over his shoulders and headed outside. "I'm going to milk the cow. I'll be back in about ten." He slammed the screen door as he left the house, chuckling to himself. His little schoolmarm was more of a prude than he'd realized.

Anna could breathe again once he was outside. She carefully poured four small circles of the batter onto the greased skillet and watched over the pancakes ready to turn them as soon as the bubbles began to form. She couldn't stop thinking about how sexy her new husband had looked with no shirt on, and she realized that she really should try to stop thinking of him as anything other than her employer. When she thought of him as her husband, it brought back their kiss in the schoolhouse, still the only real kiss they'd shared.

Ernie stomped down the stairs and stopped beside the table. "I'm hungry." It was quite clear he hated asking her for anything, but he needed to eat.

Anna turned to him and smiled. "Good morning, Ernie. Pancakes will be done in a few minutes. Go ahead and wash your hands, so you're ready to eat as soon as the food is ready."

Ernie walked toward the pail of water she had sitting on the work table. "Yes, ma'am." He didn't seem eager to do as she asked, but he didn't seem like he wanted to disobey her either. His automatic obedience was all she asked for. Hopefully he would do it with a smile in time.

She put the overflowing plate of pancakes on the table just as Jesse came in with a pail of milk. "You want me to set this on the work table?" he asked, clearly unsure of how she wanted things done.

"Let's have it with our breakfast," she suggested. "I like milk with my pancakes." She set the syrup on the table along with the butter, before taking her seat at the table with her new family.

Jesse said a quick prayer for them all before reaching out to stab one of the pancakes with his fork. He added butter and syrup before adding some bacon to his plate.

Ernie watched his father get the food, wondering if the way Anna cooked would make his father fall in love with her. He had decided to call her Anna, because it didn't feel right to call her Mrs. Hoover. That had been his mother. He wasn't about to call her ma, either, because it would feel as if he were taking something from his mother.

Jesse gave him a look. "Eat up, boy. You're working with me today, since there's no school, and I need you to have plenty of energy to help me get some of those fences mended." He knew Ernie wanted to spend more time working with him whenever he could and with school out, it would be a good time.

Ernie's face perked up at the idea. "I don't have to stay home today?" He practically bounced in the chair at the idea of helping his father for a change.

Jesse shook his head. "Nope. I can use the help."

Anna looked at Jesse, nervous about broaching the subject she knew she needed to discuss with him. She'd seen several fights about money between married couples when she'd boarded with families. "I need to go into town for supplies today. We're almost out of flour and sugar, and I want to buy some fabric to make some new clothes for Ernie. His pants are all too short, and most of them are torn."

Jesse nodded slowly. "I guess that's all right. Can you hitch up the team yourself, or do you need help?"

Anna stared at him with surprise. How would she have ever learned to hitch up a team. She'd barely touched a horse in her entire life. They simply weren't available at the orphanage. "I'll need help. Hitching up teams wasn't something taught to girls in the orphanage where I grew up."

Jesse shrugged. "I'll help you hitch them, but you'll have to have whoever's around later unhitch them. There are usually men all over this place." He still wasn't certain what each man on the ranch did for him, but they all seemed to be working all the time. He'd get a handle on things soon, he hoped.

She nodded, agreeing to ask whomever she needed to ask. She wasn't sure if she should ask him for money or if that would seem like she was out of line. As she was debating what to do, he added, "There's money in my bedroom on the dresser. Grab what you need."

Anna smiled, letting out a sigh of relief. He didn't seem to be as close fisted as the other men she'd been around. That was a good thing.

Once the breakfast dishes were finished, she stripped all the beds and washed the linens, hanging them to dry, taking a minute to get some money from Jesse's dresser, before getting into the wagon and heading into town. She'd never driven a wagon before either, but she'd been in enough of them that she certainly knew how.

She started out at little more than a crawl but slowly drove a little faster. By the time she got to town, she felt like she was driving at the same speed as everyone else on the road. When she reached town, she tied off the wagon and jumped down, going into the mercantile with the money she had, looking around her, trying to decide exactly what they needed. She should have made a list.

Mr. Stemmons smiled at her. "You find what you needed the other day all right? I saw you sitting with the new family at church yesterday."

Anna nodded. "I married Mr. Hoover. That's why I'm back in town today. I need to buy some flour, sugar, and some fabric for new clothes for Ernie." She was embarrassed to admit to the fast marriage, but she'd gotten the impression that was pretty normal here in Wiggieville.

Mr. Stemmons didn't even blink at her words. Obviously he thought nothing of a woman marrying a man she'd just met. "How much flour?"

He worked on getting her order together while she looked at the different fabrics available. She found a few colors she liked for new shirts, and some good strong denim to make some pants for both Jesse and Ernie. She chose some yarn as well, wanting to make scarves for Christmas presents. She'd been told Texas was much warmer in the winter than she was used to, but there were still days when it was very cold and difficult for a man to be out without his face covered to protect it from the wind.

After she'd paid, Mr. Stemmons loaded her wagon for her and she started toward the ranch. She spotted Mr. Hanson at the telegraph office, obviously sending a telegram trying to find another teacher. She just smiled to herself. She was in a better position as a ranch wife than she'd ever been in as a teacher anyway. As a mother, she hoped he'd find a new teacher soon. As a recently fired teacher, she hoped the search was long and arduous.

Lunch that day was a simple affair. She made creamed potatoes with small chunks of bacon throughout. It would be enough to satisfy her men, but was simple to cook and left her time open to do the others things she needed to do. While she worked, she thought about the circumstances she'd found herself in and made a decision. As much as Jesse didn't want a wife, she was going to be his until one of them died. She believed in the sanctity of marriage too much to be willing to settle for anything less than a lifetime with him.

She decided she would spend all her time cooking and cleaning and being the best wife she could possibly be, whether he appreciated her for her work or not. Maybe with time and patience, he would realize that she was the wife he'd needed all along and things would change between them. If not, she was more than willing to be a good wife to him. It was what she'd agreed to do, and she would do it to the best of her ability.

While they ate, she couldn't keep her mind off the kiss they'd shared at the schoolhouse. She watched his mouth as he chewed, thinking about what his lips felt like on hers. She tried not to be too obvious about it, but she simply couldn't tear her eyes away from his mouth, wanting it to be on hers again desperately.

Jesse felt Anna's eyes on him throughout the meal, wondering what had come over her. She had never watched him the way she watched him then, and it made him more than a little uncomfortable. At one point, he caught her eye and raised an eyebrow questioningly. She blushed pink and looked down at her plate, but the next time he looked up, she was staring at him again.

As soon as they were done eating, Ernie rushed off to play for a few minutes before he returned to work with his father. Jesse stood, placing his hat on his head as he headed for the door. Before he reached it, he turned to her, finding her still watching him. Instead of speaking, he walked back to her and grabbed her to him, crushing his lips down on hers.

Anna clung to his shoulders, thrilled to finally be kissed by him again. As long as he showed her some affection, she felt like she had some hope. He let her go as suddenly as he'd grabbed her, and she stood with her back against the work table, her breathing uneven. *What was that about?*

Jesse strode from the house, refusing to look back, because he was afraid if he did, he would drag her off to his bed. The woman played with every one of his senses, making him feel like the lowest form of a worm, because she made him feel like a man for the first time in years. He wanted to remain true to Deborah in every way, not spend time pining after his new wife. He had to get hold of himself.

Anna stood motionless for several minutes, wondering what had come over Jesse. The kiss had been so out of character for him, that she truly wasn't certain how she should react. Should she kiss him when he returned for the day to welcome him home from work? Should she pretend nothing had happened? She thought about it for a moment before deciding to follow his lead. He knew what he wanted from her, even if she didn't.

She forced herself to return to work, knowing that she had several things left to do, but for the remainder of the day, her mind was on her husband and the kiss he'd shared with her.

Before the men were done with work for the day, she'd replaced all the linen on the beds and scrubbed the upstairs of the house. She felt like she had everything in order for her friend to visit the following afternoon. She was pleased with the day's work.

Jesse stalked toward the house at the end of the day, determined not to even look at his pretty little wife. When he stepped in the door, the smells from the beef stew she had made for supper filled the air. He inhaled deeply and closed his eyes glorying in the scents. He wished she was a bad cook, so he wouldn't have anything to like about her, but she just kept disappointing him.

He walked to the basin and washed his hands, not paying any attention to her.

Anna watched Jesse carefully as he came in the house, wishing she knew the right way to act after the kiss they'd shared. Did the kiss mean he wanted her to share his bed now? She didn't know, but she would if he wanted it. Somehow she'd always been afraid of the marriage act, but with him? It seemed like something she wouldn't mind too much.

She set the big pot of stew on the table, hoping this time she'd made enough for them to have leftovers for lunch the following day, and set down the fresh rolls she'd baked that day. "Where's Ernie?"

He shrugged. "He had to feed the cows before coming in to supper."

Anna frowned. She felt very strongly that meals should be at a set time, and Ernie being late upset her more than it should. She recognized that it really wasn't the fact that Ernie was late for the meal that was upsetting her, but that it was how uncomfortable she felt with Jesse. She didn't care though. "I serve supper at five. He should be in here and ready to eat at five."

Jesse's eyes met Anna's for the first time since he'd walked in the door. "Are you telling me that my child shouldn't have to do his chores?" Why did she suddenly think she had the right to dictate to him? Was it because he'd kissed her?

"I'm telling you that I expect everything to be sitting at the table ready to eat at five. I work hard to make certain everything is ready by then so the two of you can eat on a schedule. Not coming home when you should is unacceptable. It will make the food that I worked very hard to fix cold."

Jesse walked toward Anna coming close to her and staring down into her blue eyes. "Really? You do realize that this is my home, and he's my son?"

Anna took a step closer bringing them chest to chest. "We're married and that makes him my son as well. I'm the one cooking and cleaning so this is my home. I want him here eating by five." She knew she shouldn't be so bold as to call his home hers, but she was so angry she couldn't stop the flood of words flowing from her mouth.

"And you think you should get your way with everything you do, don't you? What kind of orphanage brings up a woman to be so spoiled?"

She couldn't believe him. How dare he accuse her of being spoiled? And just think, she'd thought about sharing a bed with him earlier! "Orphanages do many things but they do not spoil children. I was anything but spoiled. I had almost no free time as a child, because we were always required to work to grow our own food. I spent the winter months cooking and sewing, and the summers weeding and planting. Ernie has had more free time in the last week than I had in my entire childhood. I ask for only one thing from you, that you be here on time to eat supper every night and you bring Ernie with you. That's not too much to ask, and you know it as well as I do!" Her voice was getting louder with each word, until she realized she was all but yelling at him. She couldn't recall anyone in her life ever making her as angry as the man standing before her.

"You have no right to tell me what I should and shouldn't do for my son. I love Ernie, and I don't care a whit what you think about him or anything else. He's mine."

She wanted to hit him. "It's not easy suddenly having a wife with a brain, is it? Was your first wife so blindly obedient that she had no mind of her own?" Even as she said the words, she knew she was overstepping her bounds, but she couldn't call them back. He had to realize she was her own person with the capability of thought. Whatever else happened between them, he would respect her.

He couldn't believe she would say such a thing about Deborah. "Don't mention my first wife to me. You know nothing about her."

"I know she was a perfect wife in your eyes. How do I become perfect? Stop thinking? Just say so. I'm sure I can figure out how to shut off my brain."

He was so angry he couldn't see straight. "You have no right to even speak her name or refer to her in any way. I will not tolerate it."

Anna glared at him. "I have a right to talk about anything I want to talk about in my own home. If I'm going to be compared to her every day for the rest of my life, I need to understand the comparison at least."

"There *is* no comparison." He turned and walked to his chair at the head of the table and sat down, not looking at her as he waited for the others to join him at the table.

Ernie rushed into the house then, throwing his coat onto the floor and flying to the basin to wash his hands. He didn't notice the anger between the adults, but sat in his chair and looked at Anna expectantly. "What's for supper?"

Anna sighed, refusing to let her anger with his father affect how she reacted to Ernie. She wanted to be a good step-mother to him, even though neither Ernie nor his father seemed to want her to fill the role. "Beef stew and rolls."

"Smells good." The words came reluctantly from Ernie's lips. She could see that he really didn't want to say them, but he felt like he should.

"Thank you. I think it will taste good too."

She took her seat, serving the stew for everyone. She'd already poured water for them all, so she looked at Jesse, and he immediately bowed his head to pray for them.

"Lord, thank you for this food. Please help us all to learn to get along with each other in our strange new family situation. Help me to control my temper in dealing with my new wife. I know that sometimes I say things I shouldn't, so please help me to work on that. In Christ's name we pray. Amen."

Anna's eyes met his, and she nodded slightly, recognizing the prayer for the only apology she was likely to get for his temper. "Did you get the fences finished today?" she asked. She knew she needed to say something to break the solid wall of ice that seemed to have formed between them.

He shook his head. "The fences all around are in bad shape. I think I've finished the worst of them, but I still have a lot of work to do on them. It sure helps when Ernie is there to hold the wire while I pound the nails, though."

Ernie didn't look up, but Anna could see the pride on his face at his father's words. "I'm glad he was so helpful today." She smiled at Ernie. "I have something I need you to do for me this evening. I need to measure you for the new clothes I'll make."

Ernie wrinkled his nose. "New clothes?"

"You've either outgrown or have holes in everything you wear. It's time for me to rectify that." She wasn't asking him, she was telling him, and she hoped he would recognize the difference.

"Do I have to, Pa?"

Jesse held back the laugh at his son's obviously sad tone. He remembered hating to stand still to be measured for clothes as well. "Yes, you do. You need to obey Anna just like you would me."

Ernie let out a loud sigh. "Yes, sir."

After the cake was served and the dishes were done, Ernie obediently stood on a chair next to the table while Anna measured him and made notes on each of the measurements. "I'll start sewing tomorrow so you can have new clothes to wear to church on Sunday."

Ernie didn't say anything, but the interest on his face showed her that he would be pleased to wear clothes that fit properly now that the hard part of standing still to be measured was over.

After he'd gone up to bed, Anna sat at the table, carefully cutting out several pair of pants for him and some new shirts, using an old pair of pants and an old shirt as a pattern, and simply adjusting them to the new measurements she'd taken. It was while she was working that Jesse sat at the table with her and cleared his throat.

Anna looked up, half afraid of what he would say to her. Jesse was sometimes friendly, sometimes cruel, and sometimes simply indifferent. She never knew what she'd get from him.

"May I tell you about my first wife so you can understand just a bit better?" Jesse asked, deliberately keeping his voice soft. He'd thought about having this conversation with her since his prayer at dinner, and he knew it was necessary for them to have simply to keep the peace.

She nodded, dreading his words. What would he say to her?

He took a deep breath. "When I first saw my wife, we were both children. I knew from the first day we met that I wanted to marry her." He frowned, thinking about how ornery he'd acted as a result of that. "I chased her around the playground at recess and made her life difficult. The other girls teased her about me, but I didn't care. We started courting when she was sixteen, and I was eighteen. I couldn't get her pa to let her step out with me before that."

"I don't really blame him. I don't think girls should marry before they're eighteen anyway."

"Well, we married a year later. She was seventeen and I was nineteen. She got pregnant with Ernie right off, and it was a difficult delivery for her. The midwife said that we shouldn't have any more babies, because she was just too small, but when she got pregnant again five years later, I was sure everything would be all right." He ran his hand over his face as if he was trying to keep from crying. "She died giving birth, and the baby died with her. I lost my wife and my daughter on the same day."

"I'm so sorry." And she was. She felt horrible for what had happened in his past, but she truly felt like he should still be able to live his life.

He shook his head. "I don't expect you to feel sorry for me. I just need you to understand why I can't love anyone else. You see, I promised her as she was dying that I'd take good care of Ernie and little

Abigail, who was still clinging to life. When Deborah died, I just lost the will to love anyone. She was my everything."

Anna cocked her head to one side. "If you had died first, would you have expected Deborah to remain faithful to you for the rest of her life? Or would you have wanted her to find someone else to make her happy?"

He stared at her for a moment and shook his head. "She'd have had to marry someone to provide for her and the children. A woman can't provide for a family on her own."

"And a man can't provide for a family, keep house, and cook. You think you should be able to do it all, but you don't think that she should have had to do it all. Why is that?"

"I'm a man."

Anna's eyes widened in surprise. Had he really just said that to her? "So it's because you're a man that you're able to do more than any woman ever could?" Did he have any idea just how he sounded?

"Well, of course." Jesse watched her face and realized he'd made a mistake. "Well, no, but I couldn't ask her to be unhappy just because I died first."

"But you think she'd ask it of you?"

He thought about that for a moment. "She'd never have asked it of me. I ask it of myself."

"Why?"

"Why? Because it's the right thing to do." Suddenly, he wasn't certain any longer that it was the right thing to do. Anna made sense, and he didn't much like it.

"The Bible says you're free to remarry if your wife dies. Why do you hold yourself to stricter standards than Jesus would hold you to?" She wasn't trying to be contrary, but she really didn't understand his reasoning.

He stood. "I don't think I can explain it in a way that you'll really understand it." He couldn't even explain it to himself any longer. She was shaking his entire belief system, and he wasn't happy about it.

"I'm going to tell you now that in the unlikely event that you fall in love with me, and I die, I will want you to remarry and fall in love again. You can't raise Ernie alone. You need help." She nodded at the pile of clothing pieces in front of her. "Did you even realize how badly he needed new clothes?"

"You can't fault me for that. I've done my best by him." He'd noticed the boy's clothes only when they'd gotten ready for church on Sunday mornings. He'd always promptly forgotten when they returned home.

Anna nodded emphatically. "I know you've done your best by him. God meant for every child to have two parents for a reason. I don't think men are meant to notice things like their children's clothes. Women do it without thinking."

He sighed. "You may be right." He turned, feeling like their discussion had been a waste. She still didn't understand, and he wasn't certain he did any longer either. "I'll see you in the morning."

She watched him walk away, wondering if anything she'd said had gotten through to him. She appreciated how loyal he was, but he took it too far.

Chapter Seven

WHEN ANNA GOT UP THE following morning, she immediately felt a sense of hopelessness. How was she ever going to be able to convince Jesse that she was good enough for him to love when he'd made his vows to a dead woman?

She sighed as she quickly dressed and hurried down the stairs, determined to cook for her new family. Julia had promised to stop by that day, and she was glad she was going to have some time to just sit and talk to her friend. Yes, Julia was coming so she could help her get the house in order, but she'd done most of that the day before. More than anything, she needed her friend's company. If she insisted, they could spend some time working on the new clothes for Ernie, but she wouldn't mind if they just sat and talked.

She quickly made up dough for bread, before toasting what was left of the bread she had on hand. She made fried eggs and bacon to go with the toast, and had everything waiting when Jesse and Ernie descended the stairs.

Jesse took a long look at Anna before he took his spot at the head of the table. He had been up most of the night thinking about her words, and it looked to him as if she'd been up a great deal of the night as well. He hated that he was making her feel badly because of his belief that he couldn't love again, but he didn't want to give her false hope.

After their prayer, he said, "Breakfast looks good." He smiled at her kindly trying to communicate without words that he was grateful for all she did for him and Ernie.

She nodded, giving him a half smile. "I hope it tastes good too."

"I'm sure it will. You have a real knack for making anything taste good." He wasn't just flattering her. He'd honestly never met a better cook in his life.

Anna nodded, shrugging slightly. "I always have. It was something I was known for back home." Why was he being so nice all of a sudden? The man didn't seem to know whether he hated her or wanted to be her best friend.

Jesse felt something strange happen in his stomach. He knew that she referred to Massachusetts as her home out of habit, but he didn't want it to be her home. He wanted her to think of his ranch, with Ernie and him, as her home. Would she ever be able to do that without them having a real marriage? And why did it matter to him so much? He shouldn't care, should he?

He cut his egg with his fork, using his toast to sop up the yolk. He liked eggs a great deal and as many times as he'd tried, he'd never mastered the art of a perfectly cooked egg white and a runny yolk, which was how he preferred to eat them. He ate a piece of bacon while watching Anna. She seemed a little cold this morning, and he couldn't help but wonder if it had to do with his talk with her about Deborah the previous night.

"What are your plans for the day?" he asked.

She shrugged. "Mostly the usual. I'll do some baking this morning because Julia is coming over for tea this afternoon. She was going to help me get the house in order, but I've done that, so I'll have her help me with some of the sewing I'm doing for Ernie." She didn't want him to think she was planning on doing nothing all day.

Ernie made a face. "I like my clothes. They're comfortable."

Anna smiled at the boy. "I'm not going to make you church suits or anything. I'm making the same kind of clothes you already wear, but they'll be the right size, and there won't be holes in them. Trust me. You'll be happy." She thought about the yarn she'd purchased to make socks and scarves for him as well, but she didn't want to mention those, because they'd be Christmas gifts.

"Do I need to take a sandwich with me for lunch?" Jesse asked. He didn't much like the idea of not seeing her at lunch time, because he enjoyed taking a break from work. He enjoyed seeing her too, but he couldn't even admit that to himself.

She shook her head. "No, not at all. Julia's not going to be here until one, so I'll be able to feed you and then spend time with her." She took a sip of her milk before asking, "What about Ernie? Is he staying home with me today, or do you need him on the ranch again?" She really wanted Ernie to go with him so she could have a private conversation with Julia.

Jesse looked over at Ernie. "I have some more fences to mend. You up to do another day of man's work?"

Ernie nodded eagerly. "I'm a little sore from the hard work yesterday, Pa, but I'm happy to do it again."

Jesse smiled as he nodded at the boy. "Then you'll go with me again."

Anna stood and cleared the table. "That sounds good to me. I'll have lunch ready at noon as always." She walked to the work table with her back to them and started washing the dishes. She wanted Jesse to believe that his words the previous evening hadn't hurt her at all. They had, of course, but she didn't want him to know it.

After the men left, she hurried through the morning's baking, wanting to have a cake for dessert for dinner, but also some cookies to share with Julia. She'd never had a friend visit her before, as strange as that seemed. Elizabeth had visited once when she lived in Massachusetts, but that had been more of a business call than anything else. She was really looking forward to spending an afternoon with her friend where they could talk about anything they wanted to talk about.

By lunchtime, she knew without a doubt she'd gone more than a little overboard on baking cookies. Not knowing her friend's favorite, she'd made six different flavors. She laughed as she looked at the dozens of cookies all over her kitchen table. She'd have to send most of them with the men, because she knew that she and Julia would never be able to make a dent in that many cookies. They'd enjoy having the snack while they were working, though.

She hurried to clean up the mess she'd made and fixed lunch for the men, glad they were there to eat the extras. The loaves of bread she'd baked were laid out prettily on the counter.

"Any reason for me to stay around while your friend visits?" Jesse asked, eyeing her carefully. He knew there probably wasn't, but he wanted to at least offer so she'd know he was available for whatever she needed.

Anna shook her head. "I don't know what kind of reason you're imagining, but I assure you, I can spend the day with my friend without causing any problems."

She'd just finished the lunch dishes and sat down to work some more on Ernie's pants when there was a knock at the door. She put the fabric pieces on the table and rushed over to the door, smoothing her apron and patting her hair. She had to laugh at herself as she did, because she was acting more like a woman expecting a beau than a woman waiting for her friend to come.

"Julia. I'm so glad you came!" She opened the door wide, letting her friend into the house.

Julia looked around her and smiled. "Your house is beautiful and spotless. I thought I was coming over to help you get this place into shape."

Anna smiled. "Well, I hurried to get it all done, because I knew it would be more fun for the two of us to sit with sewing and just spend the afternoon talking instead. You don't mind do you?"

Julia shook her head. "Not at all if you don't mind letting me help with your sewing. I certainly didn't bring any. I'd feel guilty if I spent an entire afternoon with idle hands."

Anna led her friend to the kitchen table and handed her the shirt she'd quickly basted together for Ernie. "I've got that basted, if you'll just sew it for me, I'd appreciate it."

Julia looked down at the shirt and nodded. "My mother took in sewing in the evenings, so I helped her with it a lot. I know what I'm doing with a needle and thread."

Anna smiled. "I've been sewing since I was a small child. It's one of the ways we were trained at the orphanage." From the age of five on, they'd been expected to do everything they could to pull their own weight. Anna had been pleased to learn what she could and know she was helping out.

"So how's married life? Are you and Jesse getting along better?" She had the shirt in her hands and was carefully plying the needle and thread, working quickly with even stitches.

Anna shrugged, picking up the pants she'd been working on. "I don't know. Jesse is...odd. I know he's attracted to me. When he kisses me, I can feel it inside him. But...he's very careful to always tell me that he's not going to fall in love with me, and we can never have a real marriage. He seems to all but worship his late wife, which makes me sad. How can a man feel that much for a woman who's been dead for three years?"

Julia frowned. "He's kissed you again? Not just in the school house?"

"Yes, he has." Anna blushed. "He seems to be overwhelmed with emotion, and he kisses me, but then he always regrets it." She hated that he'd never once kissed her because he liked her. He always seemed to have an ulterior motive.

Julia sighed. "How do you get along otherwise? Do you fight a lot, or do you think you're compatible other than *physically*?" She blushed as she said the last word, obviously thinking of her relationship with Tom.

"We get along fine. He's always complimenting my cooking and other things I do around the house. He seems to be happy with my skills as a wife, even if he isn't happy with me as a woman."

"Do you want to know what I think?"

Anna looked at her, her eyes filled with questions. "What's that?" She desperately needed advice from someone, and she had no one to turn to but Julia. She could always write Elizabeth, of course, but it would take a month to get a response.

"I think he is very happy with you as a woman. I think he's afraid that if he gets too close to you, he'll immediately fall in love, and he doesn't want that to happen."

Anna shook her head. "I don't think so. Wouldn't he just tell me that?" Why would Jesse complicate things?

"No, because he's a man, and they have to complicate every little thing. For some reason, they can't just come out and admit that they're attracted to you, but I certainly don't know why." Julia shrugged. "I'm so glad Tom isn't like that."

Anna smiled, knowing her friend thought she'd married the only good man who was worth anything. "I'm glad you and Tom are so happy."

Julia smiled. "Oh, we are." She leaned forward as if to impart a secret, even though no one else was around to hear her. "I'm expecting."

Anna put her sewing down and hugged her friend. "Oh, that's wonderful! Did you want to have a baby right off?"

"I never really had a chance to think about what I wanted, but I'm certainly not unhappy about it."

"I'm really happy for you! We should celebrate. I baked cookies, and I can make tea. Or would you rather have milk?"

Julia smiled. "Let's do milk. The mid-wife is certain that expectant mothers shouldn't drink tea, although she can't give any real reason why it's bad." She shrugged. "I'll listen to her because I want a healthy baby, and she has more experience than I do."

Anna jumped to her feet and brought back two glasses of milk and a big tray of cookies and two small plates. Julia stared at the cookies in surprise. "How many people were you expecting?"

Anna laughed, blushing a bit. "Well, I love to bake, and I couldn't decide which kind I wanted to bake today, so I made a bit of everything. I may have overdone it a bit. I had to send a lunch pail full with Jesse and Ernie today as well."

"I would say you overdid it just a bit." Julia laughed. "But I'm hungrier than I've ever been, so I won't complain. I wake up in the mornings, and nothing will stay in my stomach, and by noon, all I can think about is eating. I make up for the fact that I didn't eat breakfast three times over. I swear, I'm going to be bigger than a pregnant heifer by the time I'm ready to have this baby." She patted her still flat stomach fondly.

Anna could see her friend didn't mind a bit that she was going to be big. She could tell the other woman was feeling secure in her marriage. "I'll send some home with you. I've heard ginger is good for stomach ailments and there are some ginger snaps in there. I'll make sure you take some home."

"Thank you." Julia concentrated on her milk and cookies, smiling happily. "These are really good. You're going to have to teach me to bake. I'm hopeless at most domestic chores. When you first came to live with us, I was certain Tom was going to find some reason to divorce me so he could marry you."

Anna laughed. "Tom and I wouldn't have been a bit happy together. He intimidates me to the point I want to hide from him all the time. You and Tom are a much better match than he and I would have been."

"You think? I can't imagine anyone not wanting to be married to Tom. I think he's just about perfect. You almost sound like you prefer Jesse."

Anna nodded emphatically. "Oh, I do! I think Jesse is very handsome and even intelligent when he's not being deliberately bull headed."

Julia smiled. "Tom is never bull headed."

"Yes, I know. Tom is the perfect man." Anna rolled her eyes. "Tom is bigger than an oak tree. I need a man who doesn't intimidate me."

"I can't imagine Tom intimidating anyone. He's so sweet and gentle."

Anna didn't say anything else, because she was certain her friend wouldn't believe her at all, but she didn't think Tom was gentle or sweet. He'd been ready to get rid of her from the day she'd come to Texas.

They finished their cookies and talk turned to the townsfolk while they worked. Anna told Julia how terrible Mr. Hanson had been to her and about how Jesse had stood up for her. They sewed while they talked, and when Julia stood up to go, she folded an almost finished church shirt for Ernie. "You just need to do the buttonholes." She leaned forward as if to impart a secret. "I hate buttonholes."

Anna smiled. "I think all women do! I'll get them done, though." She put the finished pants on the table. "I can do those up after supper tonight, and he'll have new clothes for church on Sunday."

"You're going to be a great mother to him," Julia said as she headed for the door. She turned and hugged Anna tightly. "I'm so glad we're friends. I needed someone here who I could really confide in."

"Oh, me, too! I've never really had a close girl friend. All of the others at the orphanage paired up with best friends, but I was so quiet, that I really never did quite fit in."

Julia's eyes danced. "From what you've told me, I don't think Jesse finds you quiet at all."

Anna grinned. "I turn into something of a fishwife around him. I'm not quite certain why." She watched as her friend walked away, stopping to wave when she reached the road. Closing the door, she walked to the stove and the pot roast that had spent the afternoon cooking. She just needed to peel some potatoes for mashed potatoes and add a jar of carrots for a vegetable. The bread she'd baked while she worked on the cookies that morning still smelled wonderful.

She quickly washed the dishes from her time with her friend and set aside her sewing. She'd have Ernie try everything on after supper to make certain she'd fitted it to him correctly, but she was pretty certain the clothes would fit well. Good. She needed to show Jesse she was a good wife, no matter what he may think.

ANNA WAITED UNTIL AFTER breakfast the following morning to take Ernie aside and ask him a question. "What did your parents like to do together?" she asked.

Ernie looked at her with surprise, obviously not expecting that question. "I don't know. They did parent stuff, I guess."

Anna sighed. "Well, did they go for long walks together? Did your ma sing for him? Did they dance together?"

Ernie studied her with a blank look for a moment, and then his face lit up with understanding. "They liked to go for long rides. They'd leave me with my grandma, and they'd ride for hours. Mama was a great horsewoman."

Anna nodded thoughtfully. "Okay, thank you." She'd never been around horses much, and really was more than a little afraid of them. How was she going to be a good horsewoman? She needed to find someone who could teach her to ride. There were enough men around the ranch that could do it, she was certain, but how would she get up the courage to talk to one of them?

Ernie left with his father, and soon after he'd gone, Anna saw the same man she'd met the first day she'd come to the ranch. She was washing the dishes and staring out the window, as she often did, watching what was happening on the ranch. The cowboy looked as if he'd been born in a saddle, and she wondered if he'd teach her. She didn't remember his name, and truthfully couldn't remember if she'd ever known it. She dried her hands on her apron and rushed out the door to where the man was in the stable, feeding the horses.

"I'm afraid I didn't catch your name the other day," she said, startling him away from his work.

He looked at her for a moment before continuing to feed the horses. "I caught yours. Mrs. Hoover, boss's wife. Whatcha need?" He kept his words short and to the point, obviously not wanting to get caught talking to the boss's new bride.

Anna smiled. "I want your help in doing something to surprise my husband," she answered softly.

"What would that be?"

"I want to learn to ride. I've never been on a horse." Truthfully, she'd never touched one. She'd only driven a wagon once, and that was just that week. Riding a horse wasn't something she'd even contemplated. It seemed too complicated to her.

He eyed her up and down for a moment. "How's the boss feel about it?"

She shrugged. "I want to do it as a surprise for him. He likes to ride and it's something we can do together."

He looked skeptical. "I dunno. I don't want to get in trouble. He's a good man, and I don't need to lose my job."

"You won't lose your job. I promise."

He sighed. "Well, if you want to learn to ride, I do have a mare you could use. She's old and docile."

"She sounds perfect! I can't pay you extra, but I'll bake you some cookies," she offered. She could probably find some money to pay him as well, since she still had her savings, but because he'd be doing it during work hours, she didn't think that would be right.

He nodded. "That'll do."

"When can we start? I was thinking maybe we could do it after lunch in the afternoon while my husband is on the range. He never comes back in the afternoon until it's time for supper." She smiled at him cajolingly. "Oh, and I need to know your name. I don't know that I caught it that day I first came here." She was ecstatic to have found someone to help her.

"It's Ace, ma'am." He looked up into the rafters of the stable, as if he was contemplating her words. "Yeah, I'll do it. I'll start coming by as soon as I see him leave in the afternoon, and we'll work for an hour. No longer than that, because I've got other chores to do."

She held out her hand to shake his. "That sounds perfect, Mr. Ace. Thank you."

He spit into the dirt at her feet before taking her hand and shaking it. "Not Mr. Just Ace."

She nodded and hurried into the house, knowing that she had a lot to do as well. She didn't want Jesse to think that she wasn't doing everything she could to give him a full day's work.

As soon as lunch was over, she rushed out to the corral beside the stable and met Ace there. He looked nervous as he stood holding the reins of a thin looking horse.

Anna approached slowly, more than a little nervous. She reached out a tentative hand to stroke the side of the horse's head. "What's her name?"

"It's Chili. When she was younger, she was really fast, but she's too old for much of anything any longer."

Anna took a moment to get close to the horse, learning the feel of her. "What do we do first?"

Ace eyed her skeptically. "I think today all we're going to do is get her used to you and you used to her." He handed her the rope that was tied to Chili's harness and gestured with his hand. "Just walk her slowly around the corral. Let her get used to being guided by you, and you get used to having her close." He watched as Anna did what he told her.

"Next time you might want to bring her a sugar cube or an apple. Even a carrot. She loves them all, and they're special treats."

Anna was nervous as she walked in slow circles, eyeing the huge animal over her shoulder. Were all horses this big? she wondered. She'd only really been around them when she was in a carriage or on a board walk on the side of the road. No one had ever asked her to walk with one before. She felt more than a little intimidated.

After her hour was up, Ace took the reins from her. "That's enough for today. Remember to bring her a treat tomorrow." He walked off while Anna watched, wondering if the man remembered that she was really the boss in this situation.

Every afternoon that week, they worked with Chili for precisely one hour. Anna would start out walking her and then get onto her back. Anna shook every time she got onto Chili's back and Ace would stand beside her shaking his head. "She can smell your fear."

"I don't know how to just stop being afraid," Anna would retort. She just wasn't comfortable on the horse's back. It was Friday afternoon, and he'd let her get on the horse's back and he would guide her around the corral with the rope, but he never let her try and ride on her own. She was always with him every step of the way.

After she'd dismounted she looked at Ace, who was ready to rush into the stable with Chili. "When are you going to let me ride her on my own?"

Ace shook his head. "Not until you quit shaking every time you climb on her back. She's going to throw you as sure as I'm standing here if you don't start showing a little gumption." He spit on the ground on his way into the stable, effectively dismissing her for the day.

Anna hurried into the house and washed the horse smell off of her before she fixed supper. She'd managed to finish three pairs of pants and three shirts for Ernie, and was going to have to start on Jesse's clothes next. She wished the riding lessons were going as she wanted them to, but she was too afraid to really do anything.

Her dream was to one day ride out over the land to where Jesse and Ernie were working and ask Jesse if he'd like to go for a ride with her. She somehow knew that if he saw her on a horse, his eyes would fill with love, and he'd forget all about Deborah. She sighed. She had to figure out how to stop being afraid first, though. Ace wouldn't even let her walk the horse around the corral without him being right there. She just wasn't ready.

Chapter Eight

AFTER SUPPER THAT EVENING, Jesse leaned back in his chair, watching his tiny little wife move around the kitchen doing the dishes. He had to admit Anna was the best cook he'd ever known. Even his ma didn't hold a candle to her in the kitchen, and she had finished up Ernie's clothes faster than he'd have ever imagined. His house was spotless now, and everything in it was well-run and organized. His new wife was a wonder. He was glad he had her. He just hoped he could keep from breaking her heart.

While she moved, he noticed she was moving slower than usual. She seemed to be a bit sore. "What happened? Did you fall?"

She shook her head, continuing about her work, not willing to answer him. She was sore from the time spent on horseback that week, although she knew that she couldn't tell him that. She didn't want him to know about her surprise until she'd actually gotten good at riding. "Nothing happened."

"You working too hard?" She was such a tiny little thing, and she worked like an ox. He'd never seen a woman do the kind of work that his wife did. She seemed to roll out of bed in the morning with a frying pan in her hand, and go to bed with a needle in her fingers. She never stopped, and she accomplished a great deal. One thing he couldn't deny was her work ethic.

She shook her head again. "I'm used to hard work."

"Then why do you look sore?"

She shrugged, her eyes not meeting his. She couldn't tell him about the horse. She wouldn't tell him no matter what.

Jesse's eyes narrowed when she wouldn't meet his gaze. She was obviously up to something, and he needed to find out what it was.

He wondered if she was entertaining men in the house during the day while he was gone.

As soon as the words entered his mind he dismissed them. There was no way she'd do that. She wasn't the type at all. Still, she was hiding something from him. He'd have to start coming home during the day to find out what. He didn't like the idea of his wife hiding anything.

AFTER CHURCH ON SUNDAY, Anna was talking with a small group of ladies that included Julia when she heard the scream of a little girl. She immediately closed her eyes and said a silent prayer that it wasn't Ernie making her scream. She knew better, though, because it was always Ernie making the little girls scream. Would he ever start behaving as he should?

She glanced over and saw Ernie a few steps away from a crying Susie, a frog hopping away from the hysterical girl. It didn't take a genius to realize that Ernie had put a frog into the girl's pocket. *Why? Why would he do that on such a fine day?* She had just started to feel like she was respected within the community, and Ernie did something like that.

She excused herself politely, ignoring the knowing glances of the women she'd been speaking with. She walked over to where Ernie stood, apologizing, his face red. "I'm sorry, Susie. I didn't mean to scare you." Ernie was obviously contrite for his behavior, which actually surprised Anna a great deal. He was usually rather proud of his mischief.

Susie ignored him, continuing to wail now that she realized she had an audience. One of the first things Anna had learned about Susie was that if she injured herself, she needed to be ignored or it would be made into something much worse than it actually was.

She approached, her hand going to Susie's shoulder. "Susie, calm down. Ernie is sorry, aren't you, Ernie?"

Ernie nodded emphatically. "I didn't think the frog would scare you. I heard you say that you wanted a pet, and I thought maybe you'd like a frog for a pet."

Anna turned back to Susie. "There, you see? He didn't mean to upset you." She put her arm around Susie to walk her back to her mother, planning to have a talk with Ernie as soon as they returned home, which they would do immediately. They needed to talk about it as soon as possible.

She spent a minute talking to Susie's mother, who had twin sons in her arms, and seemed a bit exasperated by the whole thing, and turned just in time to see Mr. Hanson disappear around the corner of the church with Ernie in tow, pulling the boy behind him.

Anna didn't know if Jesse had seen, but she didn't trust Mr. Hanson to be gentle with her new son, so she ran as fast as she could through the small crowd gathered outside the church, her dress hitched up above her ankles, showing a great deal too much of her calves. She was panting when she reached them.

Mr. Hanson had backed Ernie against the back of the church and was leaning over him yelling at him. "You will not continue to terrorize the girls in this community. I don't care if your father doesn't know how to raise a boy or if your new mother is a harlot. You will not behave this way!" He pulled his belt out from the belt loops as he spoke, holding it in his right hand as if he were about to use it on the boy.

Anna hurried over and caught his arm. "You will not strike that boy!"

Mr. Hanson turned to her, his face scarlet with anger. "It's none of your business what I do. This boy is a menace, and he'll be disciplined for what he's done!"

Anna was shaking, but she refused to back down to the horrid man. "He will be disciplined, yes, but he will be disciplined by people who love him. His father and I will deal with him, and you'll not touch him ever again. Do I make myself clear?"

The man raised the belt toward Anna, and she flinched as she watched it start to fall. Jesse jumped between them, the blow that was meant for Anna catching his arm. He easily took the belt from the older man, his eyes flashing with anger. "You won't find it so easy to intimidate me."

Mr. Hanson shook his head. "Mr. Hoover, both your son and your wife are causing nothing but problems in this community. Why you married that harlot is beyond me, but you need to find a better role model for your son."

Jesse dropped the belt and used his fist to hit Mr. Hanson in the nose, causing blood to spurt everywhere. The older man dropped to his knees, and Jesse took a step toward him. "Get back on your feet and fight me like a man."

Anna rushed forward, grabbing Jesse's shoulder. "No, Jesse. You can't hit him while he's down." She moved between the two men, facing Jesse, her eyes imploring him to listen to her. "We need to go home now."

Jesse was shaking with anger as he stared down into her blue eyes. He knew she was right, but he didn't care. He wanted nothing more than to beat the other man to within an inch of his life. Finally, he nodded, turning to leave the churchyard with his wife and son trailing behind him.

Anna kept her arm firmly around Ernie's shoulders as they walked to the wagon. "We'll talk when we get home," she whispered.

Jesse said nothing as he drove them back to the ranch. His face showed that the anger hadn't left, and Anna noticed that the knuckles of his right hand looked a little skinned.

When they got home, she sent Ernie upstairs to his room while she carefully used witch hazel on his knuckles. "I wish you hadn't hit him," she whispered. She wasn't telling the whole truth, of course, because seeing Jesse's fist connect with Mr. Hanson's face had been nothing short of glorious in her eyes. She had been thrilled to see it happen, and she was glad she'd been there to witness it. She was just as glad that no one else had witnessed it. She didn't want Jesse to get a reputation for brawling.

Jesse stared at her in surprise. "He called you a harlot."

Anna nodded. "He did. He's an evil old goat, but I still wish you hadn't hit him. I don't think violence solves anything."

"Sure felt good!" Jesse said with a grin.

Anna stifled a giggle. "I'm sure it did." She walked to the stove and served the beans she'd had cooking at a low temperature the whole time they were at church. "Call Ernie, and we'll have some lunch."

While they ate, Anna questioned the boy. "Were you trying to scare Susie?" she asked.

Ernie shook his head emphatically. "No, ma'am. I really did hear her say last week after the service that she's wanted a pet for a long time, but her ma won't let her have one because she's afraid that the twins will get hair all over them. So I saw that frog while I was playing before church today, and I stuck in my pocket to give her after church."

Anna bit her lip. "And she didn't like it as much as you thought she would?" It was obvious the boy hadn't had a female influence in his life for a long time.

Ernie sighed. "I'm not sure what I did wrong. I went up to her, and put the frog in her pocket and whispered, 'There's your pet.'" He looked at Anna with a confused expression. "Why did she scream?"

Anna thought carefully about how to answer him. "Well, girls are a little bit nervous about frogs and lizards and such. They don't like snakes either. She wants a kitten or a puppy as a pet."

"But her ma won't let her have one of those! So a frog should be perfect."

Anna nodded. "I can see how you'd think so, but not really. Girls just aren't partial to frogs the way boys are. I'm sorry." She looked at

Ernie who had his head bowed sadly. "Do you think Susie is pretty?" She knew there had to be more to the story.

Ernie nodded. "I think she's the prettiest girl I ever saw, so I wanted to give her something she'd like, but I did it wrong."

Anna smiled, her hand going out to stroke his arm. "You didn't do it wrong. You just didn't know she would be like that about the sweet pet you found for her. Don't worry about it, Ernie." Her eyes met Jesse's for a moment. "You know, next time you should get her a bouquet of flowers. I bet she'd like that better."

Ernie's face perked up a little. "But men do that when they court a woman. I'm too young to court her."

Anna nodded. "You are too young to court her, but you're not too young to take her flowers to apologize for scaring her."

Ernie grinned. "I can do that. Thanks, Ma!"

Anna stared at him for a moment, stunned. It was the first time he'd called her anything but Anna, and usually it was more of a 'hey you' type thing with him. She knew he wasn't even aware he'd said it, but when her eyes met Jesse's, she could tell that he'd noticed.

After lunch Ernie ran out to play, and Jesse watched her clean up the kitchen. He'd been planning on working that day, but she'd been so kind to Ernie over his little mix up with Susie, and she'd rushed to his defense with old Mr. Hanson. He realized she'd done exactly what Deborah would have done in the same situation, and he was thrilled with her. She was proving to be not only a good wife, but a good mother.

"Thanks for standing up for Ernie today. I appreciate it."

Anna smiled. "I couldn't have let that mean old goat hurt him. He's such a sweet boy." She certainly hadn't thought she'd be saying something nice about Ernie to his father two weeks before, but after getting to know him, she realized he was a good kid.

Jesse smirked at her words. "That's not what you were saying when you were the schoolteacher."

Anna laughed softly. "Well, he's better behaved now. It must be having a woman's influence in his life." She barely refrained from sticking her tongue out at him, but she knew it would be horribly childish.

"Must be. Whatever the reason, I appreciate it. You've done more for him than I ever imagined you would when we agreed to marry."

Anna dried the last dish and put it in the cupboard before turning to him. "What did you think I would do?"

Jesse shrugged. "I'm not sure. I guess I thought you'd just do your cooking and cleaning and leave raising the boy up to me."

Anna walked over to take the seat at the table that Ernie usually sat in. "Are you glad I'm helping with Ernie? Or do you wish I'd back off?" She didn't want to overstep her bounds, but she cared for the boy and wanted to help with him as much as she could.

He thought about it for a moment, not quite certain how to answer that. "You know, I like that you're so gentle with him. I needed the help. I certainly needed the help with his clothes." He shook his head. "The housekeeper I had back East kept telling me that he was hopeless, and he was going to end up in jail someday."

"That's terrible!"

Jesse nodded. "I thought so, too. I figured you'd put up with him the same way she did, because you had to. I'm glad you're kinder to him than that."

Anna nodded, her heart hurting for Jesse. "I wish you'd had someone else who could be a mother to him after Deborah died. What about your mother?"

"She helped for a bit, but she was already sickly. She died within a year of Anna."

"I'm so sorry. You've seen a lot of loss."

He studied her for a moment, overwhelmed by her sweetness. He'd at least had the opportunity to love people, something she'd never really had. "I have, but I've had the opportunity to love a lot of people as well. I can't complain." It was then that he realized he couldn't. Yes, he'd lost the woman he loved, but he'd had her for years. He'd lost his parents, but he'd been raised by them and learned about life from them. They were good people. She had no one that she'd known her entire life except people in an orphanage. He suddenly felt very sad for her.

She smiled, squeezing his hand, before changing the subject. "I made you a pair of pants and a new shirt. I used one of your old ones as a pattern. Would you be willing to try it on for me, so I can see how well it fits?"

He nodded reluctantly. "I promise you, you'll wish you had Ernie trying things on again, because I just don't like it."

She smiled. "Let me get them." Rushing to her sewing pile, she picked through the things there until she found the pants and shirt she'd mentioned. Her face was flushed and her heart was beating a bit faster than it should. She felt like something special had just transpired between them, but for the life of her, she couldn't put her fingers on exactly what it was.

ON MONDAY AFTERNOON, Anna begged and begged until Ace finally agreed to let her ride around the corral on her own. He'd led the horse every single time afraid that her fear would get her thrown.

Anna felt triumphant as she used her knees to guide the horse around the small corral, but she was shaking at the same time. She felt like she was so high up, and she knew she could be seriously injured if she fell. She couldn't imagine sweet Chili throwing her, but she just didn't feel like she was able to keep herself in the saddle well.

She was making her way around the corral slowly for the third time on her own when she saw something speeding toward her out of the corner of her eye. She gasped and lost her grip, falling to the ground and landing in the muddy corral. It had rained the day before and she found herself covered in mud.

JESSE PUT ERNIE ON the back of his horse, and made up a reason to have to return to the house. That morning he'd 'forgotten' his nails, and this time he'd 'forgotten' his water. He carried fresh water out to work with him every day, knowing that even in October, the unforgiving Texas sun could cause dehydration.

They rode back to the house, and as he got closer, he spotted something that scared him. His tiny little bride was on top of a horse in the corral, with no one close enough to catch the reins. He knew she couldn't ride. She'd admitted to him that she'd never even touched a horse. What was she thinking?

He spurred the horse on faster, determined to get to her before she fell and hurt herself. He was less than one hundred yards away when she started and fell to the side, falling into the mud covering the ground of the corral.

He jumped down off his stallion and rushed to the corral, jumping over the fence and hurrying to her side. "Are you hurt?" he asked, carefully picking her up.

"I'm fine. Jesse, put me down! I'm filthy. I'm going to have to wash both of our clothes now!"

Jesse ignored her squeals and carried her into the house, straight to her bedroom. He carefully set her on her feet, undressing her down to her petticoat and putting her into her bed. He sat at the edge of her bed, ignoring her blushes. He didn't know whether they were because he'd seen her fall or because he'd undressed her, but he really didn't care. She had no business riding a horse without him there to help her. What was she thinking? "What were you doing exactly?"

She blushed, looking at the wall. "Well, I know you like to ride, so I thought I should learn."

"Why didn't you ask me to help you? Ace is a good cowboy, but he's not the man I would have chosen to teach you to ride." He wouldn't have let anyone teach her to ride. She was too small. Her bones were so slight, he was surprised she didn't snap them in half sweeping. She had no business atop a horse.

Anna frowned. "He's been a good teacher for me. I was doing just fine until you appeared out of nowhere riding so fast." She was angry now that he'd ruined her surprise, and she knew it was petty, but she'd wanted him to see her ride well, not fall off the first time he saw her atop a horse.

He shook his head. "You sure you're not hurt?"

She nodded. "I'm fine. I've been hurt much worse stabbing myself with a needle sewing."

He got to his feet looking down at her. "Well, I want you to stay in bed for the rest of the day just to make sure."

She stared at him in shock. "I can't stay in bed! Who do you think is going to cook and clean? Who's going to make your clothes?"

He shrugged. "All that can wait until tomorrow. For today, I want to be sure you're not hurt. Stay there until I get home." He strode from the room, closing the door softly behind him, not giving a thought to her disobeying him. What was Ace thinking? He'd go give the cowboy a piece of his mind before he went back to work.

Anna watched him as he left the room, and laid there for just a minute, confused. After a moment, she got to her feet. She had landed on her behind, and she knew she'd be sore for a day or two, but the ignominy was much worse than the injury. She would be fine, and she'd show him.

She waited until she was certain he'd left the house before getting dressed to go cook dinner for them. She'd promised him fried chicken, and he'd wrung the neck of one of the pullets that morning so she could make it. She was excited, because she knew her cream gravy was something he would immediately love. As she dressed, she laughed to herself. He'd take one bite of the gravy and fall to his knees in awe of her, begging her to stay with him forever and be his real wife.

She shook her head, wondering what her problem was. She'd fallen off a horse and landed on her behind, not on her head. She couldn't even say she'd been thrown. What was wrong with her anyway?

Chapter Nine

WHEN JESSE WALKED INTO the house at five as usual, he expected to have to fix a meal himself. He was already thinking about frying some bacon and toasting some bread, making bacon sandwiches for everyone. He'd take Anna hers on a tray, showing her that he cared if she was hurt or not. He knew he was often cold to her, but she was proving to be a sweet and caring wife, if not loving.

He stopped short just inside the door as the smell of fried chicken infiltrated his nostrils. His eyes scanned the room and landed on his sweet wife, out of bed and putting dinner on the table.

Anna turned toward the door and smiled at Jesse. "Everything's done. Just wash up, and we'll be ready to eat."

Jesse said nothing as he walked to the basin, trying his best to hold his tongue and not unleash the anger that was filling him up. What was she thinking getting out of bed when he'd carefully told her not to? What was wrong with that woman? Did she think she was invincible?

Anna ignored the look on Jesse's face, knowing he was angry with her, but refusing to acknowledge it. "How was your afternoon? Are you done with the fences yet?" She asked him the same question every afternoon, because she knew he was getting close to finally finishing.

He took deep breaths, and didn't answer her, instead sitting at the head of the table as he fought to control his anger.

Anna sighed, looking down at her plate. Ernie sat between them not noticing any of the friction between the parents. He waited for a minute and finally said loudly, "Can I just pray so I can eat? This food smells too good to just look at it."

Anna's eyes met Jesse's, hers filled with laughter, but he simply frowned at her before nodding to Ernie. "Of course, you can. I'm hungry as well, son."

Ernie said a quick prayer, and before the 'amen' had died from Jesse's lips, he had a chicken leg at his lips. He took a big bite and smiled. "Good chicken, Ma!"

Anna smiled at the name, realizing that he had only called her 'ma' for a couple of days, and had stopped calling her Anna entirely. She couldn't be happier with his easy acceptance of her, and genuinely wished his father would accept her just as easily.

She looked at Jesse, and though anger still filled his eyes, he was obviously enjoying her chicken. When he took his first bite of her mashed potatoes and gravy, his eyes closed with delight. He said nothing, but his face softened. Maybe food was the way to a man's heart after all. She'd certainly heard people say that often enough.

After the dinner dishes were finished, she reached for the shirt she'd been sewing for Jesse, and his hand stopped her. He'd moved faster than she'd ever seen a man move to get to her and prevent her from lifting the shirt, so she knew there was something on his mind. Jesse's eyes bored into hers as he said, "Ernie. Go on upstairs now. I need to have a talk with Anna."

Ernie looked between them before shrugging. "Yes, Pa. G'night." He hurried up the stairs without looking back, obviously either oblivious to the anger the adults were showing toward one another or uncaring that they were angry.

As soon as Ernie was in his room with the door firmly shut behind him, Jesse sat back down. "I don't appreciate you getting out of bed today after I told you not to. You're too little to do the kind of work you do, and you were injured when you fell."

Anna sighed. "The only thing I injured when I fell was my pride. I've injured that before and I will again."

"I told you to stay in bed!"

Anna tilted her head to the side and studied him for a moment. "And you expect me to obey your orders without thinking? Like I was one of your cowboys or your son?"

Jesse's eyes narrowed, but he nodded. "Yes, just like that. If I say you need to spend a day in bed, then you need to spend a day in bed. Don't you think I know what's best for you?"

Anna shook her head. "Actually, no, I don't think that. I'm a strong woman, and I have a brain of my own. I knew how I was feeling after my fall. You didn't. I didn't hit my head, only my bottom."

"I want you to promise me that the next time you injure yourself, or you're sick, if I tell you to stay in bed, that you'll stay in bed."

Anna glared. "If it doesn't make sense for me to stay in bed, then I won't stay in bed. Who would fix dinner if I just spent the day in bed pretending to be hurt when I wasn't? How is my work going to be done if *I* don't do it?"

"It's women's work. It can wait 'til tomorrow."

"And you would have cooked for yourself, I suppose?" Why couldn't he see that she'd done the logical thing? Why did he care anyway? It's not like she was his precious Deborah.

"I would have! I can cook eggs!" Very rubbery inedible eggs, but he didn't tell her that. He wasn't about to admit that he was a terrible cook and have her ridicule him for it. That wasn't the issue at hand anyway. "Next time I want you to do as you're told."

Anna shrugged. "I'm finding that I don't particularly like doing as I'm told. I prefer to do what seems reasonable to me. Now, if you ask me to cook something special for supper, that would be no problem. You wanting me to spend a day when I feel perfectly fine in bed? That's no logical, and I won't do it. Ever. You don't care about me except as a housekeeper anyway, so what do you care that I didn't stay in bed? You'd think you'd use your brain and be happy that I disobeyed you and you got something decent to eat!" Her voice had risen to a level that she'd never heard from herself. Was she really the one shouting at him as if he'd lost his mind?

"You promised to 'love, honor and obey' me, woman!" He pounded his fist on the table to emphasize his words.

"And you promised to 'love, honor and cherish me.' I feel no love from you! You've told me love will never happen between us. At least I married you intending to fulfill my obligations!" She got to her feet and ignored the sewing she'd planned to do. She was so angry she didn't want to have to look at him for another minute.

He grabbed her arm as she made to pass him, easily overpowering her and keeping her in place. "Why can't you just do things the easy way? Do you always have to fight me?"

"I'm fighting you? I got up so I could make you a good dinner, and you're yelling at me about it. I don't think I'm the one starting a fight here."

He sighed, pulling her to him and kissing her. At first his lips crushed hers as he kissed her angrily, but the kiss quickly turned into something else. His hands stroked down her sides and to the back of her waist, pulling her more tightly against him. He wanted her in a way he hadn't wanted a woman since Deborah died, and he hated himself for it.

For a moment, he contemplated picking her up and carrying her to his bed, but he couldn't do it. He couldn't betray his love for his late wife that way. Finally, he pulled away and stood looking down at her, his chest heaving. "Go to bed, Anna."

Before she could say another word, he'd turned away and left the room, and Anna stood watching him with her hand over her bruised lips. Why did he never kiss her except when he was angry?

THEY MOVED ALONG MORE calmly together for the next week, neither of them willing to discuss the kiss they'd shared or do anything to rock the boat. He knew that despite his growing feelings for her, he needed to have her around to cook and clean. More importantly, she needed his help parenting Ernie.

Ernie had changed a great deal in the time she'd lived with them. Part of it was physical, because he now wore clothing in good repair that actually fit him, and his hair had been cut short as it always should have been. The other part was emotional though. He truly liked Anna, and he worked hard to please her. He would never have admitted to liking her, but a couple of times he'd picked flowers on their way home from working on the ranch. He'd worked on his manners, because she'd asked him to.

Jesse was content with the changes in his son, because he knew they were changes Deborah would have approved of. The more he thought about his late wife, the more he realized that she would have loved Anna. If she could have chosen a woman to marry her husband and help raise her son, Anna would have been that woman. She would have liked her for a friend, and she would have been thrilled with how she treated their boy.

Every day his feelings for Anna grew a little more as he watched her in the kitchen washing the dishes. When she took time to read with Ernie at the end of the day. Everything she did told him that she truly cared for him and his son and made him realize that she was a good wife to him.

Finally, late on Friday of the following week, he sent Ernie home an hour early so he could take some time to think. He walked among the cattle looking over them, thinking about his Deborah. "I tried not to like her. She's a good woman, though. I think the two of you would have been friends. I feel like I'm betraying you, but then I realize that Anna was right. You'd have wanted me to love again. You wouldn't have asked me to stay single and try to raise Ernie alone. You'd have been happy with this situation, so I'm going to do my best to be the same." He took a deep breath, feeling the tears streaming down his cheeks. "I'll take things slowly, and court her like I should have to begin with. My poor Anna has never had a man act like a lovesick fool over her, and she deserves it as much as any woman would. Forgive me for moving on, Deborah, but it's the best thing for our son and for me. I'll never stop loving you."

He felt as if the words had released him somehow. A burden was suddenly off his shoulders. There were few flowers left on the ranch this late in the year, but he looked until he found some. They were red flowers that bloomed big, and he picked a few taking them to her. He wasn't sure of their name, but hopefully she would know. He wasn't certain it would matter to her.

When he got to the house, she was putting supper on the table, and Ernie was washing his hands, chattering nonstop about the day they'd had. He spoke of the work he was doing to help on the ranch, which pleased Jesse.

"Did you bring back the lunch pail?" Anna asked Ernie. "I need to wash it out so I can send you more cookies tomorrow. "I baked a cake for supper tonight, and while I was at it, I baked some cookies for the two of you to snack on during the day."

Ernie grinned. "I left it in the barn. I'll run and get it." He turned to Anna and threw his arms around her before running from the house without saying a word.

Anna stood staring at the spot where he'd been, a tear in her eye, and that's when Jesse realized that Anna truly loved Ernie. She wasn't just doing her best by him because she was supposed to. She genuinely cared for the boy.

He walked across the kitchen and held out the bouquet of flowers he'd picked, watching her take it warily. "I'm not sure what they're called, but they're pretty, and I thought you'd like them."

Anna bit her lip, staring at the flowers. "They're lovely. Thank you." But why was he picking her flowers? Did he think they would look good in the house, so he wanted them for decoration? Or did he finally decide she was good enough to be his wife?

She put them in a vase and moved them to the center of the table without asking. "They'll make a nice centerpiece for dinner tonight."

Jesse stood watching her, wishing he knew what to say to make things better between them. "Dinner smells good," he told her awkwardly, suddenly feeling shy as he realized he wanted her to be his real wife, and not just someone who cooked and cleaned and sewed for them.

"Should taste good too, I hope." He was acting odd, and she was concerned by it, but she was afraid to ask what was going on in his head. She knew she probably wouldn't like the answer.

After supper that night, Jesse offered to wipe the dishes dry, and Anna gave him a startled look. "No, thank you. I'll see to them. You work too hard all day to come home and help with my work as well."

Jesse sighed, taking a seat at the table and pulling out his knife and a block of wood. He'd been working on making a toy train for Ernie, although he wasn't entirely certain Ernie would appreciate it. He may feel like he was too old to have something that childish.

Once Anna finished the dishes, she sat down at the table opposite him, and worked on the scarf she was knitting for Ernie for Christmas. "Do you think he'll like it?" she asked, spreading it out across the table ad showing Jesse.

Jesse nodded with a smile. "He's going to love it. No one has ever taken the time to make him something like that before, well, except me, of course, but I usually just got him something from the store. I think he's going to be a very happy boy come Christmas this year."

Anna smiled, hoping Jesse liked it as well, because he was getting an identical scarf, only a bit bigger. She hoped it would get cold enough to wear them, because so far, they hadn't seen any extremely cold temperatures yet, which was probably why Texas was such a good place to raise beef cattle. "I sure hope so."

"Oh, he will. I think he realizes just how much you care about him, and he feels very secure with you around."

Anna smiled, her knitting needles flying. She worked on Jesse's gift while the two were on the range all day, and she worked on Ernie's after supper when Ernie was upstairs in his room.

When Anna stood to go to bed that night, Jesse kissed her cheek softly. "Good night," he whispered.

A few minutes later, Anna climbed into bed, her hand tracing her cheek where his lips had brushed against it. It was the first time he'd shown her any real affection when he wasn't angry. It was amazing to her that he would do such a thing.

SATURDAY NIGHT, AFTER similar treatment by Jesse all evening, Anna got up and walked down the stairs. She couldn't sleep, but she'd always had warm milk when she couldn't sleep as a child, and she was sure it would work. Something had to.

When she got to the kitchen, she quietly built the fire, and set the pan of milk on it, hoping she wouldn't wake anyone. She hadn't bothered dressing before coming downstairs, because she hadn't expected to see anyone in the kitchen.

She stood at the stove, stirring her milk before carefully pouring it into a cup and turning to carry it to the table. She was startled to see Jesse, dressed in just his work pants, leaning against the wall watching her.

She immediately felt that she should cover herself, but he was her husband. He had a right to see her if he wanted to. She rushed to the table and sat down with her milk. "What are you doing up?" she asked softly.

"I heard you wake up and came to check on you." He pushed away from the wall and got himself a cup of the warm milk from the stove. "Are you having trouble sleeping?"

She nodded. "Yes, and I thought warm milk would help, but I forgot just how much I hate warm milk." She took another small sip and made a face, wondering what had made her think she would be able to tolerate it now when she never had been able to as a child.

He moved to the table and took the seat beside hers, which surprised her. He didn't usually sit so close to her, but he'd been touching her a lot more the past couple of days, making her nervous. "I've never much liked warm milk either, but if it will help me sleep, then I need the sleep."

She sighed. "Church is going to be difficult in the morning. It's never easy to stay awake with our preacher anyway."

Jesse laughed. "I've often thought if we could find a way to store his words and listen to them later, he would be a great cure for sleeplessness."

Anna giggled softly. "That's not very nice of you."

He sighed. "Sometimes, I'm just not a nice person."

Anna's eyes met his, and she found herself more attracted to him than ever. She wanted to shout at herself to stop looking at him, because he was too handsome for her to be around comfortably without falling for, but she enjoyed looking at him. "I think you're a very nice person...most of the time."

He moved closer to her, his hand reaching out to stroke her cheek. "Anna, you're going to be the death of me. I try to be a gentleman, and you run around in the middle of the night with only your nightgown on."

She blushed. "I didn't know you'd be up, or I would have been more careful to add a robe."

He leaned toward her, his lips gently brushing against hers. "I didn't say I didn't like it."

She gasped as his lips took hers, his tongue gently invading her mouth and stroking inside to mate with hers. It was the first time he'd kissed her in tenderness, and she liked it more than she should have. Her hands moved to his shoulders and she clung to them, as she kissed him back.

After a moment, he caught her hips and pulled her to her feet toward him and down onto his lap, his lips never once leaving hers. He held her close, his hands roaming over her back and shoulders.

Anna squirmed a bit on his lap, feeling suddenly surprised that he would hold her so closely. She knew it would take a moment or two, but he would suddenly be angry with her for 'tempting him' that way.

She carefully drew her mouth from his and got to her feet. She took both of their cups to the sink and quickly washed them, fully aware the entire time of his eyes on her. What was he thinking kissing her that way in the middle of the night? "Good night, Jesse." She walked from the room to the stairs, priding herself on how calm her voice sounded. She would sleep now, and he would forget all about this by morning. She was sure of it.

Chapter Ten

MONDAY AFTERNOON, ANNA was taking dinner out of the oven and putting it on the table when there was a knock on the door. Anna sighed, not knowing who it could be at the dinner hour. She hoped whoever it was wasn't hungry, because she'd made something new for supper, and every time she did that, Jesse and Ernie devoured every morsel as if they were afraid she'd never make it again.

She rushed to the door, and opened it wide, expecting to see one of the cowhands or even Julia standing on the other side.

When she saw that it was Mr. Hanson, she wanted to slam it again, right in his face, but she didn't. She didn't invite him inside however, preferring to stand with him outside to discuss whatever he was there for. She walked outside and stepped down off the porch, turning to him. "How can I help you, Mr. Hanson?"

He crossed his arms over his chest and looked down his long nose at her. "Well, Mrs. Hoover, by acting the harlot, you have deprived my school district and the children of this community of a school teacher. I've finally managed to find another, but she won't be able to arrive until January. That's too long for the children to go without a teacher. I need you to resume your old position of teacher through the end of December until we take our winter break."

Anna blinked a few times, trying to determine if the man was serious. He was calling her a harlot in one breath and asking her to do a favor for him in the next? "No, thank you. I'm happy cooking and cleaning for my family. It's very kind of you to offer, though."

She turned to go back into the house, but he caught her arm, turning her back around to face him. "I wasn't asking you to teach. I was telling you what you would do for our community. We need you, and you will therefore, do the right thing and teach them."

Anna took a deep breath, really not believing the man had the gall to come out there an call her a harlot and demand she teach. "I don't think you understand, Mr. Hanson. I'm a married woman now. I have a husband and a son who need me home during the day so I can take care of them. Maybe Mrs. Harding will agree to do it for you."

"I wouldn't take her back. You've done a better job than she did." He shuddered. "She was kissing Mr. Harding in the street knowing she'd come here to teach. She married another woman's fiancé. No, as much as I hate it, you'll have to come back and do the work."

"I'm afraid you didn't hear me when I answered you, Mr. Hanson. I will not return to teaching. I'm happy where I am. I wish you luck in finding a new teacher who can be here sooner. I'll pray for you, Mr. Hanson." She turned to go back into the house, but he grabbed her arm once again.

This time his face was red as he leaned over her, obviously trying to intimidate her. "You will do as you're told!"

One moment he was gripping her arm and hurting her, and the next he was flying across the yard. Jesse was standing over him, both fists clenched at his sides. "Ernie, take your mother into the house."

Anna shook her head, taking a step down toward them. "No, Jesse. It's not right. I won't go teach for him again." She knew Jesse didn't want her to teach, but even more, she knew he wanted to hurt Mr. Hanson, and she wanted to distract him from it.

"Go into the house, Anna. I'll take care of this."

"No, I won't go. Please, just let it drop. Mr. Hanson, you're not wanted here. Please go home."

Mr. Hanson got to his feet, warily watching Jesse the entire time. Ernie stood beside Anna, clinging to her hand. "I'll go. That harlot of yours would probably teach all the girls the wrong things about chastity anyway." He turned his back on Jesse, who took quick advantage of the situation by firmly planting his boot in the middle of the other man's backside.

"Get off my land, Mr. Hanson, and if you ever come back, I will introduce you to the barrel of my gun just like I would any other trespasser." Jesse was shaking as he watched the older man climb into his buggy and drive away without another word.

Jesse walked over to Anna, looking at her arm where Mr. Hanson had gripped it so tightly. "Are you all right?" he asked.

Anna nodded, feeling the relief coursing through her veins. Never before had she had a man treat her as lovingly as Jesse was at that moment. "I'm fine. I'm startled by just how nasty he is every time I see him, and I'm not even certain why any longer."

Jesse pulled her to him, and Ernie disappeared into the house. "I'll just go wash my hands," he called over his shoulder. He obviously liked the idea of his father hugging his new wife.

Jesse held her tightly, kissing the top of her head. "I'm so sorry he treated you like that. I never should have left you here alone. I'm going to have one of the cowboys start watching the house during the day."

Anna sighed, rubbing her cheek against his shoulder, enjoying having someone to lean on for once. "I don't know if that's necessary. I'll just be more careful about who I'm opening the door to."

"Promise?"

She nodded. "I promise."

"I don't know what I'd do if anything happened to you. Losing my first love was heartbreaking. I don't think I could lose another."

"If you loved me that would mean something to me." Suddenly, Anna felt anger coursing through her. How dare he compare her to his first wife when he'd made it very clear he had no feelings for her at all? She pulled away from him and walked into the house, finishing putting dinner on the table, refusing to look at him at all.

Jesse watched her go into the house, knowing that he deserved the way she'd talked to him. There was no doubt about it. He hadn't been much of a husband to her. He needed to tell her how he felt, but he couldn't do it with Ernie watching. He hated to leave her angry with him for that long, but he didn't know what else to do.

As soon as the dishes were finished, Jesse sent Ernie up to bed, catching Anna's hand when she made to follow Ernie up the stairs. "You're going to stay down here and talk to me for a minute."

Anna looked down at him, the fire flashing in her eyes. "No, I'm not." She refused to listen to another word of his drivel. Pulling her hand away, she ran through the house and up the stairs, closing her bedroom door loudly. She was not going to put up with his nonsense for another minute.

Jesse watched her go and heard the door close behind her. He gave her a few minutes before following, knowing she would be even angrier if he walked into her room while she was changing. He was going to have this out with her immediately though. She needed to know he loved her and wanted her to be his real wife once and for all.

Anna had just climbed between the covers when her bedroom door opened, and Jesse walked into her room, closing it firmly behind him. She sat up in bed and gasped, holding the covers over her chest. "What are you doing in my bedroom? Get out!"

Instead of getting out of her room, he walked around to the other side of her bed and climbed in beside her, clothes and all. He'd removed his boots in the kitchen, but other than that he was still fully dressed. "We're going to talk. I wanted to do it downstairs, but you refused, so we'll do it here."

Anna stared at him in shock. "You can't just climb into my bed. We don't have that kind of marriage! You need to go!" What on earth was he thinking? He'd made the rules between them, and she expected him to obey them.

"Calm down for a minute and listen to me!" He shook his head at her, not believing that she was so angry with him when he was just trying to tell her that he loved her. What was her problem now?

"I don't want to calm down. Do you realize that every time you touch me, you end up rejecting me? I'm not letting that happen even one more time. I'm tired of you telling me I'm not good enough because you're still in love with your first wife. Do you hear me? No more!"

He sighed. "If you'll hear me out for a minute, I want to tell you that I love you, you irrational annoying woman!"

She glared at him for a moment at being called irrational, and then she slowly smiled. "What did you say?" Surely he couldn't have said he loved her and called her irrational all in one sentence. Even Jesse wouldn't do that.

"I said I love you. I've been trying to figure out how to tell you I love you for days, and you just kept turning away from me." He sighed, reaching out to stroke her cheek now that he had her full attention. "I've thought long and hard about what you said to me, and you were right. Deborah would hate it if she thought I wouldn't let myself love again just because I'd lost her. She would have loved you, everything about you. I think you would have been very close."

"And it's only how you think she would have felt about me that makes you love me?" she asked.

"Of course not! I've been falling in love with you since that day at the schoolhouse when I kissed you. Before that day, I'd kissed one woman in my life, and that was Deborah. Suddenly, I found myself wanting to kiss another woman constantly, and you were it."

Anna stared at him by the light of the moon streaming in through her curtained window. "I...I don't know what to say. I've felt like you didn't love me for so long that I have been angry with you for a while. Well, I've been angry since you started being nice. I was starting to feel as if you wanted me to fall in love with you just so you could tell me that my feelings were worthless."

His lips brushed against hers softly. "I never would have done that to you. I love you, Anna. Would you be my real wife and let me spend the rest of my life showing you how much I love you?"

Anna sighed and moved closer to him, her arms sliding around his back and hugging him to her. "I'd love to be your real wife. I...I love you too, Jesse."

He smiled, his face transformed by it. "Then why don't we get out of this tiny bed that was made for children and go down the hall to my bedroom? I have a nice big bed that's made for adults to share."

Anna blushed, but she followed him from the room. "I don't know what to do..."

He took her hand and brought it to his lips. "I will show you everything you need to know." He had a moment's worry about her getting pregnant, but he knew that what had happened to Deborah wasn't normal. She was a strong woman in many ways, and she would be a good wife for him. He would never let her go. He couldn't.

Epilogue

ANNA PATTED THE DIAPERED bottom sticking high in the air and tiptoed from the room. It was so adorable how little Katie slept every night, and she couldn't help but pat her bottom. She hurried back down the stairs to the kitchen where Jesse waited for her.

"Is she finally asleep?" he asked.

Anna nodded. "Yes. She's such an easy baby when she's awake, which is a blessing, but I wish she was easier to get to sleep. I feel like I've only slept about three hours since she was born."

Jesse smiled, pulling her to his lap and holding her close. "Why don't you sleep in tomorrow morning, and I'll make us eggs before church?"

Anna wrinkled her nose. "I've eaten your eggs before. I think I'll get up early." She stood up and walked to the table where she'd placed her paper and pen. "I'm going to bed as soon as I finish this letter. Why don't you wait for me there?"

Jesse looked at the time and nodded. "I'll do that." He kissed the top of her head. "Don't keep me waiting long."

Anna grinned at him. "You know I won't!"

She watched him leave the room, enjoying the sight of his backside as he climbed the stairs. She wasn't certain what it was, but she'd always enjoyed the sight of his bottom in his work pants.

She looked back down at the paper in front of her, finally picking up her pen. "Dear Elizabeth, I've been in Texas for over a year now. I have to say, I love it here. The summer was hot, but I've been happier here than I've ever been anywhere else in my life. Katie is getting bigger every day. I swear, sometimes it seems as if she's growing before my very eyes. I've never seen anything like it. And Ernie! I've let out his clothes just as much as I can. He's very thin, but he's going to be tall. Much taller than his father is. I'm not certain where he gets his height. He loves being a big brother. I've never seen a boy take to baby the way Ernie has to little Katie. He brings all of his friends over after church so they can see her. Oh, and remember the little girl I told you about? Susie, the one who told her parents she saw me kissing Jesse? Ernie asked her to marry him at recess one day. Ernie is only nine! Should he be obsessing about girls as much as he does? Is that normal? Well, whether it is or not, Susie agreed to marry him, and they're talking about what kind of wedding they'll have. Both know it can't happen for at least ten years, but they don't care. It's really very cute. I'm sure you're busy and don't want to read my prattle about daily life with children, but I did want to write to you and thank you. I know I didn't end up married to the man you matched me with, but without you, I'd never have made it to Wiggieville, and I'd never have met Jesse. I never imagined I could love so deeply. I wouldn't give up my life here for all the money in the world. It's a hard life, but it's a good one. Now that Katie's here, I can't imagine how I'll be able to love another just as much, but I'm sure if God sees fit to bless us with another, I'll love him or her just the same. Thanks again, Elizabeth. I'll never forget you and how you changed my life. Sincerely, Anna Hoover."

She folded the letter and set it on the work table to be mailed when she went into town the following day. She needed Elizabeth to know just what a wonderful thing she'd done for her.